THE TURCOMANS
AND KIRKUK

CONTENTS

LIST OF MAPS

Middle East

1) Middle East

(Reproduced from the collections of the Library of Congress, Geography and Map Division, Washington DC)

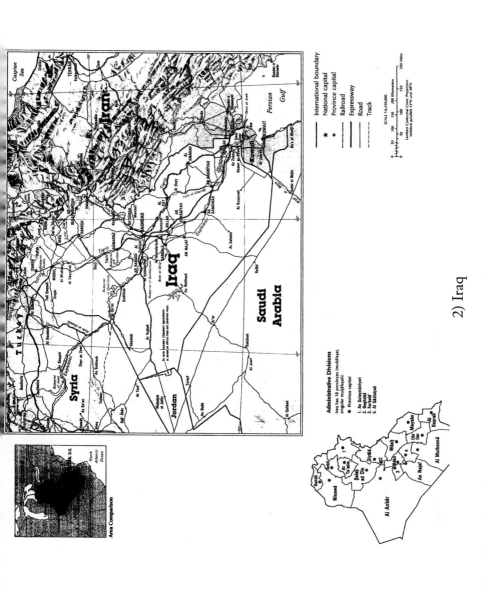

2) Iraq

(Reproduced from the collections of the Library of Congress, Geography and Map Division, Washington DC)

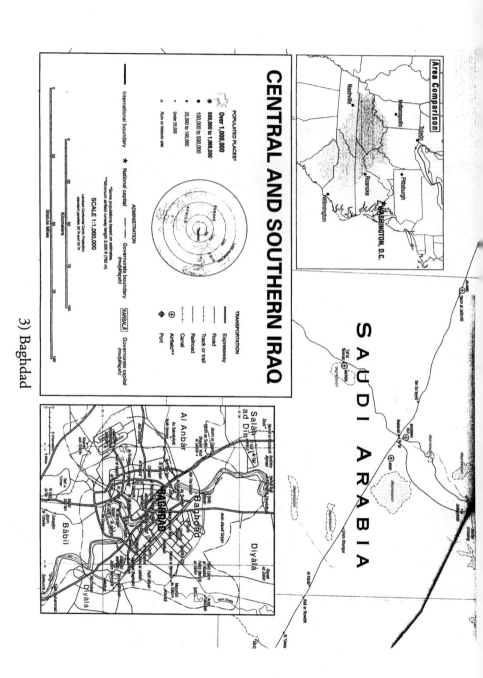

CENTRAL AND SOUTHERN IRAQ

Area Comparison

SAUDI ARABIA

POPULATED PLACES*

- Over 1,000,000
- 500,000 to 1,000,000
- 100,000 to 500,000
- 25,000 to 100,000
- Under 25,000
△ Ruin or historic site

TRANSPORTATION

— Expressway
— Road
- - - Track or trail
······ Railroad
— — Canal

ADMINISTRATION

─── International boundary
★ National capital
---- Governorate boundary (muḥāfaẓah)
⊕ Airfield**
◆ Port

KARBALĀ Governorate capital (muḥāfaẓah)

*Some populations based on estimates.
**Minimum airfield runway length 2,500 ft (762 m).

SCALE 1:1,000,000

Lambert Conformal Conic Projection,
standard parallels 30°N and 34°N

Kilometers
Statute Miles

3) Baghdad

Regional Map

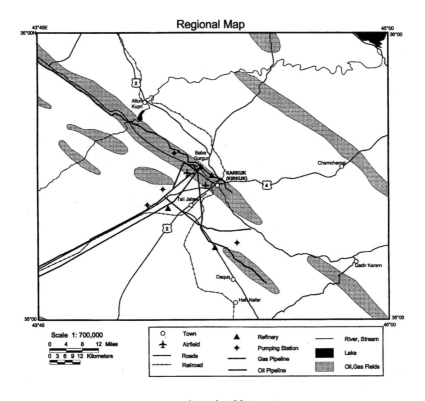

Scale 1: 700,000

0   4   8   12 Miles

0 3 6 9 12 Kilometers

○	Town	▲	Refinery		River, Stream
✈	Airfield	✦	Pumping Station	▮	Lake
	Roads		Gas Pipeline	▦	Oil, Gas Fields
	Railroad		Oil Pipeline		

Location Map

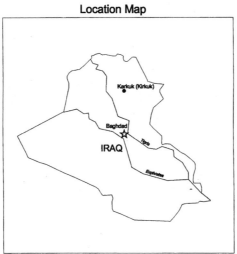

4) Kirkuk: Regional and Location

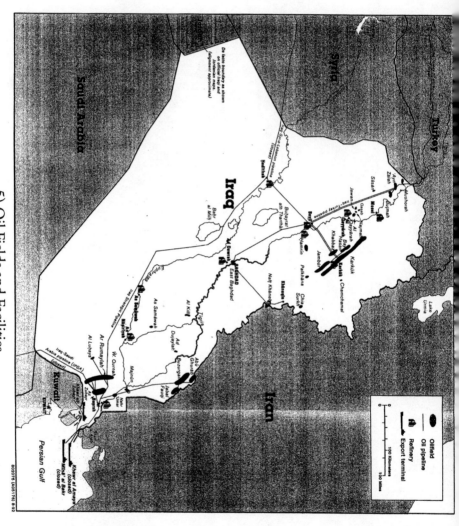

5) Oil Fields and Facilities

Oil Infrastructure

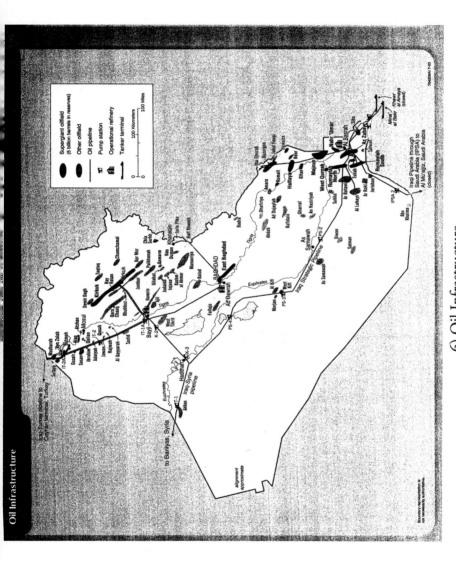

6) Oil Infrastructure

(Reproduced from the collections of the Library of Congress, Geography and Map Division, Washington DC)

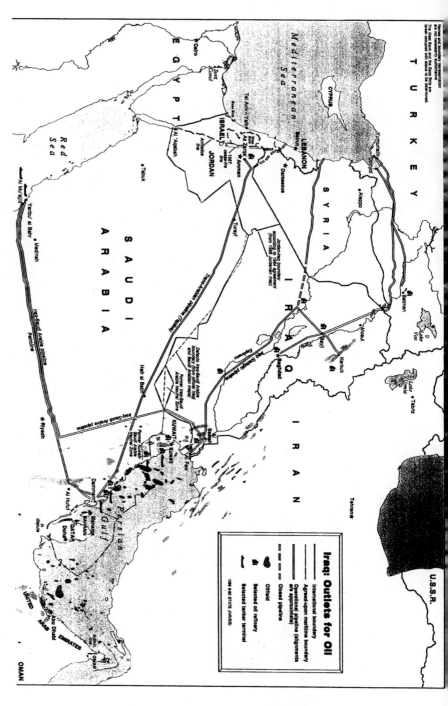

7) Iraq: Outlets for Oil

(Reproduced from the collections of the Library of Congress, Geography and Map Division, Washington DC)

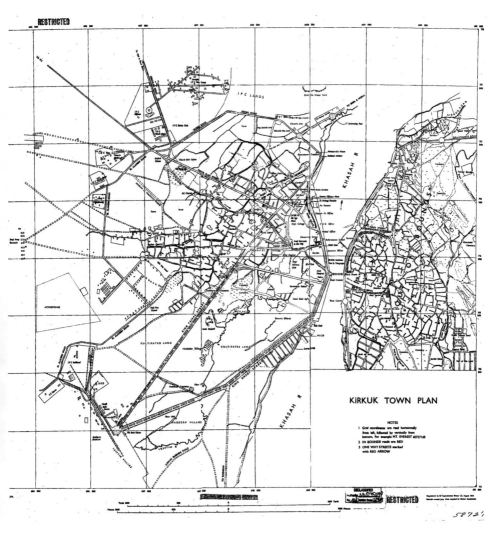

KIRKUK TOWN PLAN

NOTES
1 Grid coordinates are read horizontally from left, followed by vertically from bottom. For example MT. EVEREST 60737160
2 IN BOUNDS roads are RED
3 ONE WAY STREETS marked with RED ARROW

8) Kirkuk Town Plan

(Reproduced from the collections of the National Archives and Records Administration, Washington DC)

ACKNOWLEDGEMENTS

I AM GRATEFUL to four distinguished colleagues for their trenchant criticism and incisive suggestions on the earlier versions of this study, whose kindness and perception I shall repay by preserving their anonymity. I am indebted to Sabri Sayarı, executive director of the Institute of Turkish Studies and visiting professor at the Edmund Walsh School of Foreign Service, Georgetown University, and Soner Çağaptay, a senior fellow and director of the Turkish Research Programme at the Washington Institute for Near East Policy in Washington DC for reading the draft sections and for their invaluable recommendations. I should also like to thank Professor Eugene Rogan, director of the Middle Eastern Centre at St. Antony's College, Oxford, for helpful comments on parts of the text. Bruce Fein, a constitutional lawyer and international consultant with Bruce Fein and Associates and the Lichfield Group in Washington DC, helped me generously with information and advice in the accomplishment of this survey. I feel a special obligation to him for his interest and invaluable support. Needless to say, any errors or shortcomings in this work are solely my own responsibility.

INTRODUCTION

THE TURCOMANS CONSTITUTE an important and integral part of the Iraqi population,[1] yet there is only modest information available about them. Very little has hitherto been written about them; and a striking lack of interest in the topic on the part of non-Turkish anthropologists, historians, political scientists, and specialists in international affairs should be noted. Although there has been a proliferation of books and periodical articles, both quantitatively and qualitatively, in response to the logical deepening of concern in matters related to Iraq since the Gulf War of 1991, Middle Eastern[2] area experts have continued to shy away from the subject of the Turcomans. They have for the most part been conspicuously silent on the events surrounding Iraq's Turcomans. Apart from a few exceptions in the Turkish language, no in-depth and comprehensive historical, geographical, or ethnographical account or a social study of the Turcomans as a part of the modern Iraqi state has been published. The Turcomans are aware of these lacunae and complain of the bias of recorded history as it affects their people.[3]

Equally, the world news media and think tanks, together with most of the international nongovernmental organisations, appear to have scarcely any interest in the Turcomans. The Turcomans seldom attract attention. They seem to gain world attention and make media headlines only when brutal violence is perpetrated against them. There have been a few flashes to illuminate the scene at some given moment, but most of the time world public opinion has been kept in the dark. There has been no steady stream of news and informed comments to help highlight the plight of the Iraqi Turcomans in the way that there has been for other unfortunate peoples of the world. It bodes ill for the region's stability that virtually no one outside Turkey is conscious of the plight of the Turcomans. It is remarkable that, in a world that readily catalogues human suffering and easily assigns blame, very few have ever recognised the Turcoman predicament.

The Turcomans have been part of the urban literate classes in the region for over a thousand years. But the international community, thus far, does not seem to have even heard of the Turcomans and prefers to ignore the existence of a Turcoman reality in Iraq. The Turcomans are not put in the conscience of the people and the media around the world. This strange negligence is not easy to understand, because the international community, through choice or necessity, will continue to be intimately involved in the day-to-day domestic politics of Iraq for many years to come.

It is deplorable that most world media outlets intentionally distort the numbers and try to undervalue and underestimate the significant role of the Turcomans in Iraqi politics and society. As the Canadian best-selling author and award-winning journalist Scott Taylor points out, the Turcomans are often grouped with other communities when foreign analysts and commentators refer to the ethnic makeup of Iraq. In discussions concerning post-second Gulf war of 2003 political representation, it is common to hear specific reference made to Shiite Arabs, Sunni Arabs, and Kurds; while the remaining groups—such as the Turcomans, Assyrians, and Chaldeans—are often collectively referred to as "others."[4]

The average Western reader, as well as most of the specialists on Middle Eastern affairs, has seldom had the opportunity of gaining a thorough understanding of the Turcomans. There are numerous reasons for this lack of understanding, but three of them seem to be of paramount importance. First, as indicated earlier, there is no adequate literature on the Turcomans in Western languages; and most of what there is serves a very limited purpose. Second, it is unfortunate for the Turcomans that the West's interest in their fate has been decisively conditioned by its relations with the Kurds and the Arabs. And third, the Turcomans themselves have not always been the best spokesmen of their just, righteous, and humanitarian cause.

The Turcomans, as a distinct entity, deserve to be much better understood. This introductory study is intended to be an overdue attempt to fill a gap in that understanding. It aims to include what others have either left out or only skirted over. As the academic literature on Iraq is increasing at a seemingly exponential rate as Iraq continues to lurch towards whatever the future may hold, this country's Turcoman trouble is worth setting down in detail and putting on record. It is an area of research still unconsidered. It merits and requires serious attention. As the American Middle East analyst Michael Rubin notes, "The Turkmen have played a vital role in Iraq, and their story deserves telling."[5]

The inquiry is largely based on an analysis of American, British, and Turkish sources, as well as documents of the League of Nations and its successor, the United Nations. Some use is made of United States National Archives. Relevant British archival material, which is only available in a few extremely fragmentary and scattered forms, is utilised. The most important categories are the Foreign Office, Colonial Office, India Office, and Air Ministry files. Other British primary sources that have proved useful are private papers and diaries in the private paper collections of the Middle Eastern Centre at St. Antony's College, Oxford. Some of the source material comes from the Woodrow Wilson Memorial Collection deposited at the United Nations Headquarters Library. The work also draws on an array of secondary literature to extract the last full measure from the limited source material available.

A historico-legal methodological approach is adopted to explore the roots of the question and to draw conclusions from the general trend of politics. The investigation is concerned with underlying motives and tendencies rather than with the dramatic quality of events. Each statement of importance is made with a footnote of reference giving chapter and verse. Archival material references include file number, volume or document number, description of the document and date. Detailed bibliographical guidance is provided for those seeking to follow up on fine points or check on different interpretations.

After setting the stage by providing a brief background on the Iraqi Turcomans, the survey puts special emphasis on and devotes much space to the past and present status of the city of Kirkuk and its environs, outlines the importance of oil production and exports for the Kirkuk area and evaluates the place of the region's oil revenue in Iraqi economic development, mentions the role of the pipelines in transporting Kirkuk's crude through Turkish territory to the Mediterranean Sea coast and traces the effectiveness of the measures taken for protecting the security of these pipelines against sabotage attacks, draws attention to the policy of the central government of Iraq that the ownership of oil fields in the country rests with the entire Iraqi people and indicates that there can be no question of oil in the north being solely for the benefit of one group, examines the consequences of the international legal rights of the Turcomans, discusses the impact of the Turcoman case in its quest for justice, and reviews the gross human rights violations committed against the Turcomans. General observations and conclusions about various aspects of the issue are summarised at the end, and, finally, a concise account of the legality and righteousness of Turcoman demands is presented.

CHAPTER I

A BRIEF BACKGROUND

THE TURCOMANS, THROUGHOUT their history in Iraq, had always been and still are a positive component of society, contributing to their country with their skills and high level of education. They have helped ensure, in every aspect, the orderly administration of government under the principles of justice and equity, which they value highly. They obey the law and are willing to give service to the authorities in Baghdad. They are loyal and devoted to their country and for the most part get along reasonably well with their compatriots. The Turcomans are highly tolerant of other ethnic groups and religions, and they have always tried to exist in harmony with other nationalities who have chosen Iraq as their country of residence. As far as possible, they have avoided becoming entangled in the ethnic and religious conflicts that have plagued other communities.[6] As Iraq specialist Richard Nyrop aptly puts it, "On occasions of disputes between Arabs and Kurds, the Turcomans stood aside, seeking to avoid involvement and favouring a peaceful solution to the issue."[7]

The Turcomans have long supplied a great many officials for state service and enriched town and countryside with their quiet industry and sound sense. They had close links with the bureaucracy of Ottoman times. This, added to their industriousness, gave them an advantageous economic position. The Turcomans are a relatively well-off population. They are mainly businessmen, landowners, merchants, the middling shopkeepers, artisans, and craftsmen. Some well-known Baghdadi and provincial families are of Turcoman origin. The Turcomans created no problems in the country and did not pose any threat to the state. They do not harbour any desire to carve out any Iraqi territory either to rule independently or to be annexed to Turkey. No separatist tendency is seen among them. Preservation of territorial integrity and national unity in Iraq, as reaffirmed in United Nations Security Council's resolution 1546, is a priority for the Turcomans. They have never taken up arms against regimes in Baghdad, and their goal is only to better their conditions in Iraq. In fact, they are the only people in Iraq who did not revolt or resort to arms for their rights.[8]

According to certain authorities, the original meaning of the term *Turcoman*, or more properly, *Türkmen*, comes from the Persian word *turkmanend*, signifying "resembling a Turk." Another interpretation being from the Turkic expression "Turkmen," meaning "I am a Turk." The name Turcoman has been used since the fifth century, first by the Iranian historians Gardizi and Abul Fadl Baihaki in the same sense as the Turkish *Oğuz*. The Turcomans are also cited in the Chinese encyclopaedia of the seventh century. In Arabic geographical literature, the Turcoman is first mentioned by Muhammed Ibn Ahmed al-Mukaddasi in the tenth century. It has been used almost synonymously with the terms *Türk*, *Oğuz*, or even *Kıpçak*. Whatever the original meaning, the term is generally understood to refer to those Altaic/Turkic peoples whose members associate themselves with Oğuz Kağan and who speak any of the southwestern Turkish dialects.[9]

Since the eleventh century, the name Turcomans has belonged equally to all Turks who crossed the Oxus and embraced Islam, including the ancestors of the Ottomans. All these Turcomans alike were descended from the Oğuz tribe, which had previously lived in central Asia. The Turcomans were settled in Iraq before the Ottoman conquest in 1534. The first stage of Turcoman settlement in Iraq dated from the sixth and seventh centuries. The Turcomans assumed important positions in the Sassanid Empire and started to establish settlements in the hilly parts of northern Iraq. They can also be traced to Turkish garrisons established by the Caliphs in the ninth century and to immigration in the time of the Seljuks (Great Seljuks 1037-1117 and Seljuks of Iraq 1117-1194) and to Beytiğin Atabeys of Arbil (1144-1232). Turcoman migration to the region rapidly increased during the Seljuk Empire of the eleventh and twelfth centuries. The Mosul district, and even the country extending down to the north of Baghdad, was continuously owned and governed by Turks for eleven centuries. At the time of the Abbasid Caliphs, these lands were in the hands of Turkish governors and soldiers and were of a Turkish population. These Turkish governors enjoyed complete independence and sovereign rights. In the last millennium, the Turkish dynasties of Atabeys and Artuks founded six Turkish states in the region. After these dynasties, the Seljuk Turks made themselves masters of Mosul; they considerably embellished and increased it and made the town the centre of a high civilisation. It was only after the Seljuk Turks that the Ottoman

Turks ruled over these lands. The Turcoman population in this area thrived during the Ottoman era.[10]

The Iraqi Turcomans keep their solid character and their Turkish speech. It appears to most competent observers that the Turcomans, as a people, possess sound moral virtues. Faruk Sümer, perhaps the most noted authority on the history of the early Turkic tribes and confederations, states that they are, for the most part, good-natured, prudent, earnest, and hospitable even to their enemies. Honesty, sincerity, love of freedom, respect for their elders, absence of cunning, and pluck in a dangerous moment are predominant features of their character.[11] Richard Starr, director of the American archaeological team that conducted excavations at Yorgan Tepe near Kirkuk between 1927 and 1931, described the Turcomans, based on his eyewitness experiences, in the following glowing terms: "In the region of Kirkuk the Turcomans predominate in the main. God has made of them steady and willing workers. It has also given them a serious, contemplative, stolid state of mind particularly conducive to careful work. The Turcomans who made up the greater part of our working force were, on the whole, honest, interested, and capable workers, when properly trained and decently treated. They responded with loyalty and enthusiasm to fair treatment."[12]

The Turcomans are fond of poetry, music, and singing. They have a long oral and written tradition of epic and lyric poetry. The oral tradition played a significant role in the continuation of folk poetry through centuries. The Turcomans retain their own customs and unique folklore, which are quite different from those of other ethnic communities. The status of women in Turcoman society is high. Veiling and seclusion, forced marriage, marriage without previous acquaintance, large age differences between spouses, polygamy, and male privileges in divorce are not common among Turcoman society. Despite the supremacy of Arabic, the main language in which teaching was allowed in Iraq, Turcoman literature has preserved its originality and developed and contributed to the consolidation of inner and heartfelt national sentiment.

Possessing a deep sense of their own identity in relation to the surrounding Kurds and Arabs, the Turcomans are well educated, and the national consciousness is strong among them. They share close historical, social, and cultural ties with their kinsmen in Anatolia. They are mainly Sunni, middle class and urban, and lead a sedentary life. The Turcomans are primarily a settled people. Despite often temporary migration for work and military service, most Turcomans continue to live in the same regions as their forefathers.

The majority of the Turcomans keep religion a private matter. The fabric of the Turcoman community is civil and mainly secular. Most of them advocate the separation of state and religion in post-war Iraq. Secondary school graduates usually prefer to continue their higher education in Turkish colleges and universities. During their education in Turkey, they see, of course, the workings of the modern and exemplar Turkey. They entertain admiration and respect for the progress achieved by Republican Turkey.[13]

The Turcomans live in compact masses in northern Iraq, mainly in the areas of Kirkuk, Arbil, Talafar, Kifri, Daquq, Altın Köprü, Tuzhurmatu, and Kara Tepe. This region includes the bulk of Iraq's northern oil fields, and Iraq's main oil pipelines run through the middle of the Turcoman strip. In addition to these historically Turcoman-populated districts, there is also a sizeable Turcoman presence in the capital city of Baghdad—mostly concentrated in the northeastern neighbourhoods of Adhamiyye, Raghiba Khatun, and Waziriyye. The estimated number of Turcomans living in Baghdad is about three hundred thousand. Turcoman emigration from Iraq has become common. Repression at home and the appeal of greater opportunity have drawn large numbers of Iraqi Turcomans to Turkey, where they have established numerous associations and cultural foundations. The oldest Iraqi Turcoman association, Iraqi Turks Culture and Solidarity Association, was formed in 1958 in İstanbul. Türkmeneli Co-operation and Cultural Foundation, a nonprofit organisation, was established in 1997 in Ankara to unite support for the Iraqi Turcoman community within Turkey. The Turcomans are becoming increasingly visible and vocal in Turkey.[14]

The two words, *Turks* and *Turcomans*, mean one and the same thing. The Turks in Iraq are of the same stock as those in the Republic of Turkey. Indeed, they are called Turcomans only because the British, in creating 1920s Iraq, wished to separate them from the Turks in nearby Turkey as an early census-rigging ploy. This was all the rage at the time, as the fledgling Soviet regime under Vladimir Ilyich Lenin also went about subdividing their own Turks into Turcomans, Azeris, Uzbeks, and the like. Subsequent Iraqi regimes followed the pattern with forcible reeducation programmes to persuade the Iraqi Turcomans that they were a mere subtribe of Soviet Turkmenistan.[15] Nothing could be farther from the truth.

The difference between the Turks of Iraq and the Anatolian Turks, which the British sought to establish by calling the former Turcomans, had no foundation; in fact, such a position was quite indefensible. It was claimed by the British that the Turkish language spoken in Iraq was not identical to that spoken in İstanbul; but was there in Anatolia a single spot where the same

Turkish was spoken as in İstanbul? In fact, the dialect used by Iraqi Turks was the same as that spoken in Anatolia; the difference between them was less than that which existed between French spoken in the north and that spoken in the south of France.[16]

In commenting on the Turcomans in 1963, Stephen Hemsley Longrigg, the British political officer in Kirkuk between 1919 and 1922, and a veteran of twenty years' service as an executive of the Iraq Petroleum Company, has written: "Turcomans are hardworking and law-abiding, cultivators and townsmen, self-contained and politically unambitious, and providers (above all those from Kirkuk) of far more than their proportion of government officials both in Ottoman and in present times, they have preserved their identity against Kurdish and Arab neighbours. Feelings of attachment to İstanbul or Ankara are not unknown. The leading families stood high with the Ottoman authorities, from whom many held fiefs which became nineteenth-century estates."[17] In very many respects, Longrigg is correct. His realistic views were informed by a great deal of direct personal experience.

The size of the population of Iraqi Turcomans is open to speculation. Population statistics are woefully inadequate in Iraq, and they suffer from an overall dearth of itemised and comparable information. Specific details of population composition are unavailable, and even the estimates of total numbers are subject to wide error. Iraq, until now, has had six censuses: 1947, 1957, 1965, 1970, 1977, and 1987. Of these, the only one considered reliable is the 1957 census. Detailed data have been released slowly, and only in 1959 were the complete results published. This census, the only one in which Iraqis were allowed to declare their mother tongue, revealed that the Turcomans, after Arabs and Kurds, were the third largest ethnic community, numbering 567,000 out of a total population of 6,300,000. The importance of the 1957 census lies in the fact that this was the first and last Iraqi census that allowed the Turcomans to register as Turks. This point is not mentioned in any of the extant literature describing the period. In later censuses, the Turcoman category, under the section of nationalities, was dropped. Using the above figures, and taking into account that the annual population growth rate among the Turcomans is a minimum of 2.5 percent, the Kirkuk-born and Kirkuk-raised Turcoman scholar Erşat Hürmüzlü, meticulously calculates that presently they constitute not less than two million, or around 8 percent of an estimated Iraqi population of twenty-five million.[18]

This is, with a fair degree of accuracy, clearly a reasonable and minimum number. Some leading Middle East analysts, such as Yossef Bodansky, who has been director of the United States Congressional Task Force on Terrorism and Unconventional Warfare for more than a decade, even say that the size of Iraq's Turcoman population may be as high as two and a half million.[19]

According to the estimates of the United States-led Coalition Provisional Authority, however, the Turcomans represent less than 5 percent of the Iraqi population. The basis for this erroneous estimate originates from the sources that represent the information gathered by the Baathi government, which sought to eradicate the Turcoman presence in northern Iraq. Based on those figures, the Turcomans were given just one of the twenty-five seats in the Iraqi Governing Council. This figure is unrealistic by all accounts and does not correspond with the facts. Instead of having at least two seats, the Turcomans were represented symbolically by one nonpolitical person. Every known major Iraqi political party, except the Iraqi Turcoman Front (a collection of nineteen different political parties and organisations), was included in the council. The Turcomans complained that their representative on the council did not adequately reflect their political views. Similarly, the ministerial ranks in the interim government, announced on June 1, 2004, did not reflect the country's true demographical proportions. The thirty-three cabinet members included only one Turcoman, who had been given the position of minister of science and technology. Western observers seem to take little notice of anomalies such as these, which have a considerable impact on the Turcoman community.

A federal state that simply divides Kurd from Arab will be difficult to sustain. No government in Baghdad, democratic or authoritarian, can afford to concede its authority over disputed, oil-rich Kirkuk or any other district. To do so would show weakness and risk further fragmentation. Some groups might take advantage of the new state's weakness to press for secession. Moreover, when a federation is defined as being about two ethnic groups, then clearly all the other ethnic groups, who do not have a share in the federation, are, to one degree or another, being discriminated against. Why should a Turcoman citizen have fewer rights than an Arab or a Kurd in Iraq? The Turcomans have long had an importance beyond their numerical strength. Any discrimination in favour of Iraq's two largest ethnic communities is inherently undemocratic. Many fail to see this point.

Before and since the second Gulf war, Kurdish leaders have protested that they have no interest in establishing an independent state. All they want, they say, is the same level of regional autonomy they have enjoyed since 1991. But they dismay American officials and Iraqi government members with a considerably expanded set of demands. Not only are they asking for substantial independence in internal matters, they have also been trying to annex the city of Kirkuk. Kirkuk was not part of the Kurdish region before the war; and the usually well-informed the *Wall Street Journal*, which has an important audience in both the United States and abroad, stated in an editorial on January 13, 2004, that Kirkuk cannot be considered a "Kurdish" city.[20]

CHAPTER II

THE CITY OF KIRKUK AND ITS ENVIRONS

KURDS HAVE CONVERGED on Kirkuk to claim it as their own, setting the stage for a struggle that profoundly affects the country. Kurdish representatives say that Kirkuk is part of the history of Kurds and insist that it is an ancient Kurdish city, and that is nonnegotiable. They are adamant that a Kurdish Kirkuk is immutable and irreversible. The conflict over the city is one of the most explosive in Iraq. The Kurds' demand to absorb it into their region is viewed by the Turcomans and the Arabs as a threat to Iraq's unity. Iraq's neighbours also see it as the first step towards Kurdish independence.

Kirkuk is the most important city of northern Iraq, located some 280 kilometres north of Baghdad, bounded by the Little Zab in the northwest, the Djabal Hamrin mountain range or Brown Mountains in the southwest, the Diyala in the southeast, and the mountain chains of the Zagros in the northeast. The city, sitting on the ruins of a three-thousand-year-old settlement, is separated by the broad pebbly bed of the Hasa River in a wide fertile basin beneath the Kani Damlan range. The river, which is dry except in winter, flows from the northeast and runs southwards.

The core of the old town on the left bank is the citadel, built on a walled hill or ruin-mound that rises forty metres above the plain, overlooking the rest of Kirkuk. Within is a compact mass of flat-roofed houses built of stone and *juss* mortar, divided by narrow alleyways; beyond the walls the houses have spread on to the flat land by the river. The only road for traffic skirts the town northwards from the bridge along the riverbank. The citadel contains several mosques, two arched bazaars, and a Christian church dating from the first millennium. In 1998 the last residents were removed from the citadel, and the demolition of the eight hundred fifty Ottoman-era houses on the site was completed. By then nobody was living there. The new town on the right bank is also closely built but is penetrated by two main thoroughfares—the Fatha road, which runs west from near the bridge, and the road northwest to Baba Gürgür, the headquarters of the oil fields. The present estimated population is over seven hundred fifty thousand.

Kirkuk's importance was first hinted at in the Old Testament. King Nebuchadnezzar cast the Jews of Babylon into a "burning fiery furnace," a site that some scholars believe was the endless flame from Kirkuk's natural gas. It was a clue to the oil deposits discovered two thousand five hundred years later. Kirkuk commands the oil field. This productive field extends from southeast to northwest along the line of the Kani Damlan hills and the Avana Mountain on both sides of the Little Zab. The oil occurs in a thick porous and fissured limestone. Thick marls lie below, and the oil is capped by a group of red, green, and grey silts and marls with thin limestone bands and layers of anhydrite and rock salt embedded. The structure is an elongated dome about a hundred kilometres long and varies from one to two kilometres wide, sloping fairly steeply on the southwest, more gently on the northeast, and almost level on the top. Along the axis are three slight humps: the most important at Baba Gürgür, the central at Avana, and the third at Khurmala farther northwest.

Oil is present for about eighty kilometres, and gas escapes in the Khurmala dome. Kirkuk sits atop an ocean of oil holding 40 percent of Iraq's huge reserves. The zone owns 5 percent of the oil reserves in the world. Measured by the wealth of the oil resources beneath it, Kirkuk is perhaps the richest city on earth. As Milan Vesely—a commentator on current Middle Eastern affairs based in Washington DC—remarks, "Supposed to be the key to the region's future, it is a relatively simple matter to raise this 'black gold' to the surface, but getting it to the refineries and pumping stations where it can be turned into cash in the bank is another thing altogether."[21]

A great oil industry has grown up round Kirkuk since the first gusher was struck nearby at Baba Gürgür on October 14, 1927. John Randolph, the American consul in Baghdad, reported that the first well immediately began to flow at the rate of 95,000 barrels a day. The gusher flooded the countryside with oil for nine days before workers could bring it under control. The well was shut on October 22, 1927, and arrangements were made to pump the oil, which had been stored in a ravine, back into the well. Precautions had been taken against fire, but indications of heavy rain occurring before all the oil was disposed of would have made it necessary to burn off the oil in the ravine, to prevent damage to cultivation had the ravine become flooded. The ravine when emptied was sanded over.[22]

The formation of the Kirkuk field was such that the oil flowed at an even pressure without pumping and could be simply regulated by the control

settings at the wellhead. Kirkuk has since become the centre of activities for
the Iraq Petroleum Company, an Anglo-French-Dutch-American consortium.
Oil seepage and natural gas leaks have been common in this area for centuries.
Vast reserves of oil are so close to the surface that one area has been on fire
since antiquity because of natural gas escaping from the ground.

Kirkuk put Iraq on the world oil map. The area remains a giant. Kirkuk
is a key to the economy in the north. The city holds the richest wells in the
country. There is such abundance in Kirkuk that when an international
nongovernmental organisation began digging two water wells in 2004 as
part of a rehabilitation scheme in the destroyed village of Kara Hanjir, it
struck oil. Kara Hanjir is about ten kilometres east on the road from Kirkuk
to Chamchamal. Kirkuk has produced fourteen billion barrels over the years
and still has an estimated ten and half to twelve billion left.

Before the second Gulf war in Iraq began, many policy makers and
oil industry experts believed that Iraq's oil industry would recover and
provide most of the funds needed for the country's reconstruction. Such
optimism was unwarranted. More than three and a half years after the Baathi
regime collapsed, the performance of Iraq's oil industry is far below prewar
expectations. Looting, sabotage, neglected infrastructure, and mismanagement
have all curbed production and kept major oil companies away from Iraq.
With demand for oil soaring due to the Asian economic boom, the need for
Iraq's oil is more pressing than ever. What makes the disappointment with
the Iraqi oil industry's failure so deep is the scope of potential oil resources
that rest beneath its sands.[23]

Of all the oil-producing countries, Iraq is perhaps the least explored.
Only 10 percent of Iraq has been explored. Only seventeen of eighty fields
discovered and evaluated in Iraq are operating, most of them clustered around
Kirkuk in the north and Rumaila in the south. Two decades of isolation have
taken their toll. Virtually no exploration has occurred in recent years, and
what little has was without the benefit of sophisticated exploration techniques.
Such potential wealth might catapult Iraq to a high place in the list of major
oil-producing countries. With political stability and sufficient investment,
it is predicted that Iraq may be able to bolster production to as much as six
million barrels per day by 2010 and eight million barrels per day by 2020. To
ramp up production to such levels, Iraq will have to attract billions of dollars
in foreign investment, a level contingent on achieving better security.[24]

At present, oil output from Kirkuk is averaging around five hundred
thousand barrels per day. Kirkuk's current dominant place in Iraqi oil
production reverses pre-first Gulf war production patterns, when the southern

Rumaila fields were responsible for nearly two-thirds of Iraqi oil production. Production in southern Iraq was particularly affected by destruction caused by this war and has not recovered from the blow. The quality of Kirkuk's oil is also significantly higher than that of the southern fields (lower density and lower sulphur content), and production is less plagued by problems such as water intrusion into the oil reserves, a major problem in the south. Under optimal circumstances, Kirkuk oil could be very attractive to foreign investors because of its low production costs and proximity to the Mediterranean Sea, giving easy access to major European markets.

According to the United States Energy Information Administration's report on Iraq published in July 2005, Kirkuk export crude quality has declined since the second Gulf war to around thirty-two to thirty-three degrees API, while sulphur content has risen above 2 percent. The report also said that overpumping on Kirkuk in the months leading up to the United States' invasion in 2003 and poor reservoir management practices during the Baathi era—including reinjection of excess fuel oil, refinery residue, and gas-stripped oil—"may have seriously, even permanently, damaged Kirkuk. Among other problems, fuel oil reinjection has increased oil viscosity at Kirkuk, making it more difficult and expensive to get the oil out of the ground."[25]

It is well worth remembering that British and French companies considered the possibility of building a pipeline, linking the oil fields of northern Iraq, through Turkish territory to the Mediterranean Sea board as early as the 1930s. In a United States Department of State memorandum dated March 16, 1933, it is mentioned that the British Oil Development Company considered the construction of a pipeline from oil fields in northern Iraq to Alexandretta (İskenderun). Of course, this route was much shorter than the Kirkuk-Haifa line under the process of construction by the Iraqi Petroleum Company. It was understood that the British Oil Development Company had called upon its constituent companies for capital to carry out its development. The British, Italian, and Swiss companies had supplied the capital requested; but the French company was still negotiating.[26]

The American ambassador in Paris reported on January 27, 1937, that there was a plan under consideration by the Compagnie Française des Pétroles for the possible construction of a new pipeline from the northern Iraqi oil fields across to Alexandretta. But this plan was in a vague state and might not be developed for years to come.[27]

The Iraqi Petroleum Company intended to construct a pipeline from the oil fields of northern Iraq through Turkish territory to a Mediterranean terminal in 1956. Iraqi Petroleum Company officials had broached the idea of such a pipeline for the first time with the Turkish prime minister Adnan Menderes in August 1956, and it had been favourably received. There were no physical difficulties about a pipeline through Turkey. The Iraqi Petroleum Company had, however, been deterred from starting this project by shortage of capital and of steel pipe. But the importance of this route seemed likely to grow further in the future. A pipeline running from Kirkuk to the Persian Gulf was not considered an attractive or economic proposition.[28]

Turkey and Iraq are neighbours and have always been close partners on issues such as trade and economic cooperation. Turkey provides a natural export outlet for Iraqi oil. Despite security problems—which have resulted in the killings of more than one hundred Turkish citizens, most of them truck drivers—Ankara's economic interaction with Iraq is sustained in its natural course, and trade continues to expand. The number of Turkish deaths exceeds the military casualties suffered by most of the members of the multinational force in Iraq. Turkey serves as a crucial humanitarian and economic hub for Iraq. All kinds of assistance and supplies freely flow from and through Turkey into Iraq to find their way into Iraqi households as well as many vital sectors of the economy: Turkey supplies electricity to help overcome the energy shortage and is exploring the possibilities of further increasing this item.

Turco-Iraqi economic relations are developing. In November 2003 the two countries signed an electricity cooperation protocol, and in August 2004 they discussed transboundary waters and the opening of a second border crossing, while concluding the first postwar contract for export of northern crude oil from Kirkuk. Over one thousand Turkish firms are active in Iraq, primarily in construction and transport, with Turkish trucks bringing in tons of goods for the inhabitants. Bilateral trade has reached two billion United States dollars in 2004 and grew further in 2005. It is estimated that Iraq spends at least two and a half billion dollars a year on importing oil products, with the demand for gasoline rising sharply and existing refineries still subject to interruptions caused by sabotage of oil pipelines. In efforts to meet the increasing demand, Iraq sought in August 2005 to import an extra 12,500 barrels (two million litres) of gasoline from Turkey per day. Commercial exchanges can be much augmented by opening a second border gate at Ovaköy. This would ease the burden on the existing Habur Gate, which suffers from severe bottlenecks.

Turkey and Iraq signed an agreement on August 27, 1973, in Ankara under which they decided to build a 1,126-kilometre crude oil pipeline from Kirkuk to Yumurtalık on the Mediterranean, at a cost of 350 million dollars. The agreement came after several years of negotiations, which had in the past been hampered by Turkish apprehensions concerning political instability in

Iraq. The pipeline was to have an initial capacity of twenty-five million tons of crude a year when the first stage was to be completed in 1977, and this capacity would increase to thirty-eight million tons a year by 1983. Turkey was going to take 40 percent of the pipeline throughput to meet its own crude oil needs, and the rest would be exported. The agreement stipulated that Iraq would lay 474 kilometres of the pipeline and Turkey the remaining 652 kilometres. The main attraction of the pipeline to Iraq appeared to be that it offered an alternative cheap route for crude to the Mediterranean, in case the Syrian route was closed. Another attraction of the Turkish deal was that it guaranteed a market for 40 percent of the pipeline throughput.[29]

Turkey would be able to meet all its crude oil needs through the pipeline and was scheduled to buy ten million tons a year of the twenty-five million tons to be pumped initially. Turkey and Iraq were to share the cost of construction and maintenance in proportion to the length of the pipeline in their territories, which made Turkey's share about 200 million dollars. It was reported that the total cost might be 50 million dollars more than the 350 million dollars originally estimated. Turkey was to receive thirty-five United States cents a barrel as rent and loading expenditure. Estimated income to Turkey, when the pipeline would be operating at a twenty-five-million-ton capacity, was put at over sixty million dollars a year. The pipeline would terminate with offshore facilities and include five pumping stations, three of which would be in Turkey. The two stations in Iraq would be at Kirkuk and in Jazira; and those in Turkey at Mardin, Bozova, and Osmaniye. The planned pipeline would therefore run from Kirkuk parallel to the Tigris River and then across the Tigris and parallel to Turkey's southern border to the Mediterranean.[30]

On January 3, 1977, Iraq opened an oil pipeline with a capacity of thirty-five million metric tons per year, which ran from Kirkuk through southeastern Turkey to the port of Yumurtalık on the Mediterranean coast. Yumurtalık is a town on the western shore of the Gulf of İskenderun, to the east of the mouth of the river Ceyhan. The capacity of this pipeline was expanded in 1983 by increasing the pumping stations and using chemicals to ensure augmented flows. Throughput capacity was increased from thirty-five million tons a year to forty-nine million tons. Near the Yumurtalık terminal the pipeline's eighty-kilometre diameter was enlarged. A twenty-kilometre stretch was widened to forty inches (a hundred centimetres), and a sixty-kilometre stretch to thirty inches (seventy-five centimetres). Five pumping stations were built, two in Iraq for the State Company for Oil Projects and three in Turkey for BOTAŞ.[31] A second crude oil pipeline running parallel to the first one across Turkey was commissioned on July 27, 1987, boosting total export capacity by one-third. It had a capacity of 500,000 barrels per day. It increased Iraq's oil exports through Turkey to 1.5 million barrels per day. In addition to laying pipe, the work included building five pumping stations, five 135,000-cubic-metre oil storage tanks at Yumurtalık, and six 65,000-cubic-metre tanks at Kirkuk.[32]

The Turco-Iraqi pipeline agreement of 1973 stipulates a minimum annual revenue to Turkey whether the line is used to the full capacity or not. Therefore, it is most advantageous for Iraq to use that route to the optimal level, with due consideration to the agreement with Turkey. Yumurtalık is an ideal terminus for an oil pipeline from Kirkuk. The cheapest and most economical method to bring down the oil from northern Iraq is to build a pipeline from Kirkuk to Yumurtalık and transport the oil from this port across the Mediterranean to Europe and elsewhere.[33]

On average, Iraq sent 800,000 barrels of Kirkuk crude daily through the northern pipeline before the second Gulf war, but the line has been beset by bombings since the war ended and has therefore managed only sporadic exports. Pumping of the crude is irregular, averaging around 400,000 barrels per day when the system is functioning. It is likely that exports from the Kirkuk oil field were running at around 200,000 barrels per day until sabotage in early June 2004, as a result of which, there has been only a gradual resumption of shipment through the northern pipeline. The pipeline has struggled to manage more than "testing" levels of throughflow since it was reinstated in spring 2004 after an earlier attack; it was then taken off-line again after a further attack in May. In late May, sabotage set ablaze a pipeline west of the Kirkuk oil fields, and Iraqi crude again stopped flowing to Yumurtalık. Flows to Yumurtalık had in any case been in stops starts, a problem that Iraqi officials attributed to technical problems. Sales resumed through the attack-blighted pipeline on June 23, 2004.[34]

During the evening of September 2, 2004, saboteurs detonated a bomb on the northern oil pipeline, causing a huge explosion and fire. Security officials said it was the most devastating act of sabotage since the targeting of oil facilities began in April 2003. Exports to Yumurtalık were immediately halted until further notice. The sabotage of the pipeline came as the Iraqi authorities were hoping to resume sales of Kirkuk crude on a term basis. At the end of August 2004, the Iraqi State Organisation for Marketing of Oil had sold on a spot basis one million barrels of Kirkuk crude to Turkey's TÜPRAŞ for delivery to its Aliağa refinery, and two million barrels to a Canadian refinery. Ninety percent of Iraqi government revenue comes from oil, and the flow of funds is essential to pay for the country's reconstruction.

Electricity generation, clean water systems, roads, and other parts of the infrastructure are all in need of reconstruction funds, and capital investment is a necessity. Iraqi oil minister Thamir al-Ghadhban stated on August 29, 2004, that the loss of revenue due to the sabotage against oil installations had cost the country around seven billion dollars during the past year. He explained that these losses were incurred by the suspension of oil exports, the import of oil products, the money spent on repair work, and the burnt crude oil and oil products. For every day the northern pipeline is not operational, Iraq's tottering economy loses seven million dollars. Sabotage of pipeline infrastructure continues to disrupt shipments.[35]

Officials at the Iraqi Oil Ministry announced on November 2, 2004, that saboteurs have mounted the biggest attacks yet on Iraq's oil infrastructure, blowing up three pipelines in the north and hitting exports via Turkey. The attacks, which were hours apart, sharply reduced crude oil supplies to Iraq's biggest refinery at Baiji. The Iraqi government was already struggling to build up stocks of refined oil products ahead of winter. Sabotage against oil facilities in the north and central Iraq intensified in the autumn of 2004, as United States forces attacked cities where insurgents have support. Imports of refined products have also been disrupted. The first pipeline attack on the night of November 1, 2004, destroyed a section of the northern pipeline in the Riyadh area, sixty-five kilometres southwest of Kirkuk. It was followed by two further attacks, including one in the Qoshqaya region, northwest of the city, on a pipeline connected to the Bai Hassam oil field and feeding the main export pipeline. In early November 2004 the market price of crude oil was at a near-record high of more than fifty dollars per barrel, and Iraqi and United States officials were relying on exports to help revive the country's daily export volume.[36]

On November 7, 2004 the flow of Kirkuk crude to Yumurtalık resumed and was running at about 200,000 barrels per day after repairs were made to a key pipeline that had been blown up by insurgents in the previous week.[37] The extensive fighting in six major Iraqi cities in mid-November was accompanied by a marked increase in the type and number of sabotage operations against the country's oil facilities around the Kirkuk area. The attacks aimed at oil pipelines, with approximately two hundred fifty bombings since the war in March 2003. The targets selected included oil wells and storage tanks, with almost daily attacks on pipelines. The insurgents on November 14 blew up five oil wells at the Khabbaz oil field, with a loss of capacity of around 75,000 barrels per day. Other incidents included attacks on a storage tank at the Khabbaz field; setting fire to a storage tank at a pumping station along the Kirkuk-Yumurtalık pipeline about forty kilometres southwest of Mosul near the town of Ain al-Jehash; sabotage of a pipeline at the Fatha area that feeds the Baiji refinery and a nearby power plant; and the sabotage of an oil pipeline west of Kirkuk on November 15.[38] Another well was bombed on November 16. The pumping of crude oil to Yumurtalık was stopped and then resumed after a week at the level of around 200,000 barrels per day. The Iraqi State Organisation for Marketing of Oil has accordingly cancelled several oil shipments, scheduled for late November and early December, as a result of the emergency situation.[39]

By early January 2005, Iraq's northern oil exports had remained idle for three weeks, as sabotage wreaked havoc on the area's infrastructure. Exports from the north, through Turkey, ceased from December 18 to 19, 2004, following attacks against the Kirkuk-Yumurtalık pipeline. The pipeline has been hit several times since then, further hampering work to resume flows. Oil officials in Baghdad said a restart date could not be reliably predicted. The whole system on both the refining and export side was under constant attack. Attacks against oil facilities in Iraq's north and centre, where insurgents are strongest, have been relentless since United States forces attacked the city of Fallujah in November 2004. Apart from the export revenue lost, Iraq has been hit by severe shortages of fuel and electricity because attacks have also targeted domestic pipelines, refineries, and trucks carrying fuel imports. A series of sustained attacks on domestic pipelines and power structures have forced the North Oil Company to shut down some field production, while refineries have cut throughput and power generation, and transmission has been interrupted. An explosion ripped open a section of pipeline running from the Kirkuk fields to the refining centre of Baiji on December 30, 2004.[40]

Northern pipeline was sabotaged, forcing its closure again, on February 15, 2005, some twenty-four hours after sporadic pumping had resumed following the shutdown in December as the result of a bomb attack. Shippers said that pumping had managed a flow of just over 100,000 barrels per day during the brief period that the pipeline was open. On February 16 two pipelines linking Kirkuk with the Baiji refinery were damaged by explosions, while another pipeline from Baiji to the Daura fuel refinery—the largest Iraqi producer of gasoline, kerosene, and other refined products—was attacked. A fourth pipeline was sabotaged in the Bajwan area, northwest of Kirkuk. On the same day, the colonel in charge of security in one of the northern districts was shot dead in his car in Ajeel, west of Kirkuk. Three days earlier two pipelines, one gas and the other oil, were set on fire near the Avana oil field forty kilometres north of Kirkuk.[41]

A sabotage attack on one of Iraq's northern pipelines on March 29, 2005, yet again delayed the resumption of crude supplies to Turkey's Yumurtalık terminal. An oil official in Baghdad said the latest explosion, on a pipeline in the Riyadh area southwest of Kirkuk, would further delay the resumption of exports for ten days. Since the attack on the pipeline in mid-December 2004, northern exports have remained suspended—with a string of subsequent attacks thwarting attempts to restart pumping. Since that date, all Iraq's oil sales have been exported from its two southern terminals, the Basra Oil Terminal and Khor al-Amaya. In another sabotage incident on March 27, 2005, a pipeline linking the Kirkuk region with the Baiji refinery was blown up sixty kilometres west of Kirkuk. The attack came less than twenty-four hours after the pipeline had been repaired following an earlier explosion.[42]

Repeated attacks force Baghdad to collect oil in a tank at Yumurtalık and sell it off in four-to five-million-barrel spot tenders. Yumurtalık has a tank storage capacity of 7.8 million barrels. Three wars in the last twenty-six years, the eight-year conflict with Iran, the 1990-1991 Gulf war, and the United States-led coalition invasion in 2003—plus more than a decade of sanctions and isolation—have left Iraq with an old, dilapidated infrastructure and an imperfect knowledge of the conditions of its northern oil fields. The Coalition Provisional Authority's dismissal of guards protecting oil field facilities, including pipelines, has had its toll on oil infrastructure integrity and resulted both in the delay in oil field and installations repair and frequent interruptions to the flow of oil exports. What is more, actual damage done to these facilities, including the bombing during battles in 2003 of the critical pipeline junction under the Al Fatha bridge—which has still not been repaired—has severely constrained Iraqi export potential. Experts have predicted that until these repairs are made, exports from Kirkuk to Yumurtalık, will only reach half of the levels they had achieved before the United States invasion.

Insurgents target oil in order to undermine the efforts by the coalition and Iraq's government to rebuild the Iraqi economy. The precision and sophistication of the attacks raise suspicion that former members of Saddam Hussein's Oil Ministry aid the sabotage campaign. In the months following the Baathi fall, the Coalition Provisional Authority entrusted oil security to foreign contractors. These contractors, in turn, hired tribal interests to guard oil installations at a monthly rate of over a thousand dollars per kilometre secured. This approach failed largely because the tribes began to compete amongst each other. Losers would blow up pipelines and oil wells in the territory of the tribe that won the contract in order to prove the successful bidders' incompetence. In late November 2004, responsibility began to shift

from foreign contractors to the indigenous security forces, and a special
directorate was set up at the Iraqi Ministry of Oil to coordinate pipeline
security efforts. The ministry has re-created a fourteen-thousand-strong
force of oil police to protect installations. It has signed contracts with local
tribesmen to guard oil pipelines and installations that pass through their
territory.[43]

According to Vesely, the ongoing insurgent attacks have resulted in a loss
of seven to twelve billion dollars of Iraq's export revenue in 2004. Brought
down to a personal level, this meant a loss of 490 dollars to each of Iraq's
about twenty-five million citizens. He asserts that the insurgents targeting
Iraq's oil structure are well versed in how the country's dilapidated system of
pipelines and pumping stations is integrated. Crucial choke points include
the Baiji junction, where three pipelines come together, which is repeatedly
attacked; the last attack on this critical junction came only two days after
valves destroyed in a previous attack had been replaced. Each attack leaves
the overall system even more vulnerable to breakdown, thus compounding
the problems for any future elected Iraqi government.[44]

The cheapest and most effective way to protect a pipeline is to bury it or
prevent easy access by surrounding it with walls and fences. Pipes can also
be fortified with external carbon fiber wrap that can mitigate the effects of
explosive devices. Equally important is shortening the lead time between the
attack and the repair. Saboteurs often target pipelines at critical junctions or
hit custom made parts that take a long time to replace. As a result, ruptured
pipelines are often out of operation for weeks. To reduce the lead time,
pipeline operators could be equipped with sufficient repair items as well as
inventories of spare parts.[45]

It was announced that Iraq's State Organisation for Marketing of Oil
on June 29, 2005, awarded 2.63 million barrels of the four million barrels
tendered in its first Kirkuk crude tender for over a year to ExxonMobil,
Repsol YPF, and Total SA. The two European companies won one million
barrels each, with ExxonMobil picking up the remaining parcel. Bids had
been requested for one-million-barrel cargoes. The nearly loading window
prompted a wide price spread in the offers received, leading State Organisation
for Marketing of Oil to award only two-thirds of the oil on offer. Kirkuk
exports via the Turkish terminal of Yumurtalık were effectively halted in
December 2004 by a major explosion on the northern pipeline. Continued
insurgency attacks on the pipeline have allowed only sporadic exports,
allowing storage at the port to fill towards its capacity of 7.5 million barrels.
Despite continued attacks on the pipeline, Iraq's Oil Ministry is eager to go

on sending oil quietly through to Yumurtalık when possible—even at lower pumping rates than previously—and to issue tenders whenever oil stocks reach the four-to five-million-barrel level.[46]

James Glanz of the influential the *New York Times* reported from Baghdad on September 3, 2005, that the crude oil is flowing again to Yumurtalık after Iraq's government put in place elaborate new security measures and decided to move its product in what is essentially a clandestine operation. In the new export system, officials secretly open Iraq's northern pipeline to send batches of oil to Turkey and then shut it down again before insurgents can attack. The government has recruited, trained and equipped thousands of mostly Sunni Arab and Turcoman tribesmen and stationed them at hundreds of new guard posts along the pipeline. The new system for moving that oil around relies on gradually filling up storage tanks in secure areas near Kirkuk and then, at unannounced times, sending the oil in the tanks as quickly as possible through the pipelines. Still, as a result of the sporadic operation, a total of only five million barrels of oil flowed from the northern oil field to the Turkish terminals at Yumurtalık in August 2005.[47]

Despite a series of announcements that the flow of crude has been resumed, continuing sabotage attacks have consistently thwarted attempts by the oil authorities in Baghdad to intensify security around the northern pipeline. At the same time, sporadic attacks on pipelines feeding power stations to the north of the capital are continuing. Threats to oil infrastructure will remain high. Insurgents know that crude exports are the principal source of government revenue and that domestic crude supplies to local refineries are crucial for electricity generation and for fuel. As such, both have been a target and will remain a particular concern.

The sabotage campaign has an impact on Iraqi economic development. To meet its growing needs for foreign exchange, Iraq must begin to develop its untapped reserves, especially in the northern region. Under normal circumstances it takes between five and ten years to translate reserves into production. This means that investment in new capacity should begin as soon as possible so that sufficient revenues can be generated towards the end of the decade. But Iraq today is considered the riskiest destination for foreign investment of any of the world's emerging markets. Some of the world's largest international oil companies—such as ExxonMobil, Royal Dutch Shell, and Chevron Corporation—have indicated an interest in developing Iraq's oil resources; but without security and a hospitable investment climate, they are unlikely to send skilled workers and expensive equipment to Iraq or make the multibillion dollar investment required.[48]

The nameplate capacity of the Kirkuk pipeline system is 1.6 million barrels per day. Additionally, around 50 percent of Iraq's gas is located in the northern zone. The country's gas reserves are estimated at 3.1 trillion cubic feet, ranking them the tenth largest in the world. The Kirkuk region is rich in sulphur and bitumen products. Sulphur is also produced as a by-product of oil refining, Kirkuk crude having the highest quality sulphur content. The wealth of sulphur, naphta, and bituminous products contained in the soil of Kirkuk has been known and exploited since ancient times. The bituminous springs are especially well known at Baba Gürgür, where bluish flames rise out of the ground.

Kirkuk stands among gardens; orchards of limes, olives, figs, and apricots; and vineyards. The fertile soil gives good crops—rice and vegetables near the river; tobacco, cotton, and fruit in the hill country; and wheat and barley on the plains. Kirkuk is a rich agricultural region, as a result of the Iraqi government's massive irrigation projects, starting in the 1930s, on the Hawija, Qaraj, and Kara Tepe plains around the city. The chief exports apart from oil are wool, wheat, barley, fruit, gallnuts, and gum from the Kara Dağ region, and large numbers of sheep, goats, and cattle. But the chief occupations, apart from oil production, are those of mercers and drapers, Kirkuk being a distribution centre for northern Iraq. Woollen textiles, felt for coats, cotton materials, and pottery are produced. The district has abundant supplies of water. In addition to the Zab and the Tigris, there are the streams of Hasa, Daquq, and Aksu, all of which cross the area. More important are the underground rivers and also the frequent mountain springs.

Before the second Gulf war, it was guaranteed that Kurds would not enter Kirkuk or Mosul. This was agreed, as one of the principal objectives concerning the future of Iraq, by all participants at the meeting of representatives of Turkey and the United States—with delegations from the Assyrian Democratic Movement, the Constitutional Monarchy Movement, the Iraqi National Accord, Iraqi National Congress, Iraqi Turcoman Front, Kurdistan Democratic Party, Patriotic Union of Kurdistan, and the Supreme Council for Islamic Revolution in Iraq—held in Ankara on March 19, 2003. To this end, it was categorically emphasised in the seventh clause of the final statement of the meeting that "in order to help foster national unity and reflect the reality that all parts and cities of Iraq belong to the nation as a whole, in perpetuity." And in the eighth clause it was recorded that "the uncontrolled movements of refugees and internally displaced persons, and Iraqis from taking the law into their own hands or inciting civil discord were strongly discouraged."[49]

Yet after Saddam Hussein's government collapsed on April 9, 2003, thousands of Kurds moved down from the northernmost regions of Iraq, where they had lived in an autonomous enclave since 1991. *Peshmerga* of the Patriotic Union of Kurdistan poured into Kirkuk on April 10, 2003. They came to reclaim property they deemed to be theirs. Kirkuk had initially been left largely to its own devices and disorder after the fighting stopped. Kurds brazenly looted homes and business and government offices throughout the day; by nightfall the highways to the cities of Arbil and Sulaimaniya were crowded with thousands of cars and trucks laden with stolen good.[50]

The American war correspondent C. J. Chivers's lapidary descriptions of these lootings in the *New York Times* can be considered firsthand testimony. Obviously, he was a disinterested compiler of the events. As the extraordinary and vivid reports from him revealed, every car and truck was packed with stolen office furniture, air conditioners, water coolers, fire extinguishers, and more. The Kurdish guards pretended not to notice. Most cars with Kurdish fighters returning from Arab villages appeared packed with other people's household goods.[51]

Kirkuk was swept by determined, almost methodical looting by Kurds for a second day, before United States forces, waiting on the outskirts of the city, began to move in to stem the anarchy that had ruled the city since it was abandoned by the Iraqi authorities. The United States military was criticised for not filling the authority vacuum in Kirkuk, after pushing out the Baath Party rulers a day earlier. Most of the reported two thousand troops of the 173rd Airborne Brigade, which arrived overnight, remained largely out of sight in two airports on the edge of the city.[52] The following quotation from Chivers will better help set the local scene: "Widespread looting continued unchecked for a second day, occurring within sight of *peshmerga* and directly in front of the United States 173rd Airborne Brigade, which arrived to help establish law and order." And he continues, "Entire villages were looted and vandalized. Around Kirkuk, in several directions, were villages nearly emptied where the houses have been sacked. Each door opened to a scene suggesting unchecked theft and rage. Stray pieces of remaining furniture were flipped and shattered."[53]

In Kirkuk itself, the transition was proving uneasy. The combination of the undisciplined *peshmerga* and the absence of a sizeable American presence had made for at least a temporary vacuum. The city's electricity was out. Markets were closed or mostly empty. Residents complained that potable water was scarce. Arsonists had struck. In the still air of sunset in the evening of April 11, 2003, columns of smoke rose in several neighbourhoods. Kirkuk's cotton plant was ablaze.[54]

This was not all. By nightfall on April 11, 2003, the buildings of the Kirkuk-based North Oil Company—the national concern responsible for oil production in the northern oil fields, with roughly one thousand five hundred wells astride a reserve of petroleum that might be as large as ten billion barrels—were stripped; some were sacked and set afire. The plunder is outlined again by Chivers in no uncertain terms: "Windows were smashed, doors shattered, and anything, no matter its value, was game for thieves. The looters were Kurdish soldiers and civilians." The American correspondent certainly was in a position to recognise the extent of the pillage better than anybody else, and he adds, "They stacked oil company cars with ceiling fans, light bulbs, spare tires, soiled mattresses, cracked porcelain and flower pots. They tore down drop ceilings to take the aluminium and sell it for scrap. They took the computers that ran the company power plant and phone network, the trucks, forklifts and buses that tended to the oil fields, and the shelves, chairs, desks and file cabinets in managers' offices. Some Kurds drove away in cranes. The frenzy lasted two days and continued at a slower pace for a week."[55]

Hundreds of looters still showed up each day to carry away valuable pieces of the North Oil Company, nearly a week after United States troops were said to have secured Kirkuk's oil fields. The damage to the company's sprawling complex just northwest of Kirkuk was vast. Offices were stripped of equipment and phones then gutted by arson. About 180 company vehicles were lost; the looters either drove away in them, towed them, or pushed them. Electrical and mechanical workshops, where custom parts were fashioned for the well fields, were stripped as thoroughly as the Iraqi officers' club. The few dozen American paratroops on duty here protected only the processing plant of the state-owned company. They left to the whim of Kurdish guards acres of warehouses, which, before the current looting spree, had contained 500 million dollars worth of spare parts, which were necessary to resume operations. Until a week before, the company had produced a million barrels of oil a day. Oil company officials said that without the parts—let alone the fire-damaged offices and battered control boards that must be repaired or replaced—it would take two or three months to bring back the flow of light crude that was supposed to help pay for the reconstruction of Iraq.[56]

For two days the *peshmerga* systematically plundered the abandoned government offices in Kirkuk. They began immediately to burn all of the land deeds and birth registries. Their objective was to destroy or remove the records so that they could support their claim that Kirkuk is a Kurdish city. Without paperwork, there would be no proof of postwar ownership. The *peshmerga* did not limit their looting to abandoned government institutions, however; and when they stormed into a Turcoman suburb, a bitter clash erupted. In the fighting, the Turcomans managed to force the Kurds back, but they had ten killed and thirty wounded. Turcoman residents professed worries about the future. The first Americans entered Kirkuk on April 11, 2004, and order was gradually restored.[57]

Mosul descended into anarchy during the morning of April 12, 2003, with widespread looting and intermittent shooting starting as soon as the Iraqi military's 5th Corps fled. United States forces remained at points to the north, west, and east, leading to bitter complaints from frightened Arab residents who said their Kurdish neighbours were behind the pillaging. Preachers at Friday prayers in Mosul's mosques complained about the dangerous power vacuum. The Kurdistan Democratic Party sent forces to Mosul late on April 12, 2003. Arab and Turcoman residents expressed opposition to a Kurdish move on Mosul. Kurdish residents rapturously greeted the arrival of freelance Kurdish gunmen with clapping and singing. They ransacked government warehouses and offices. Rioters also torched a central food distribution centre.[58] What happened was a complete violation of what had been agreed at the Ankara meeting of the Iraqi opposition of March 19, 2003. There was definitely a decision not to enter Kirkuk and Mosul. But when the war started, twenty thousand Kurds went into these cities, and more than half of these people settled in the area.

The chaos and looting that engulfed Kirkuk reignited fears of ethnic conflict and instability in a region where Kurds, Arabs, and Turcomans live side by side. There were signs of tension, including demonstrations for rights by the Turcomans and the Kurds' proclivity for driving down the streets in armed groups. The armed victory laps made Arabs and Turcomans uncomfortable. Mosul, a sprawling and diverse city of dizzying political complexity, was also a potential ethnic tinderbox. International displacement was now a serious problem. The Arabs and the Turcomans came under pressure from Kurdish forces to leave their homes in and around the cities of Kirkuk and Mosul. Buildings were burnt, and offices looted; and violent clashes between Arab tribesmen and Kurds, which left several dead, were reported. Entire villages were commandeered by armed Kurds, who sent scores of Arabs fleeing. The Kurds ransacked the villages, peeling off roofs, ripping out doors and windows, and looting whatever else they could. Newly displaced Arabs from these areas were once again swelling the ranks of the homeless.

Deadly riots among Kurds, Arabs, and Turcomans have already shaken Kirkuk as various groups battle for property and primacy. Tensions are continuously rising among these groups vying for control of the city. Of particular concern is the makeup of the United States-appointed city council. Originally, the council was intended to have twenty-four members, six from each of the city's four ethnic groups. But then the coalition appointed six additional "independent" members, five of whose current officers are Kurds. The council has seen bloc votes and walkouts that have frozen its work. In April 2004, the Turcoman and Arab groups jointly suspended their membership for several months.

Government jobs go almost exclusively to Kurds. The governor and the police chiefs are Kurds. Kurds are monopolising the government offices in Kirkuk; hence, all decisions have been made in favour of them. In these offices, they also enforce the use of Kurdish, even though most of Kirkuk's population do not speak Kurdish. Growing Kurdish supremacy in Kirkuk manifests itself in the renaming of streets and institutions, the flying of the Kurdish flag, the seizure of public and Baath Party buildings by Kurdish parties and organisations, and other symbolic and conspicuous measures that are deeply resented by non-Kurds. All signs in the city are being changed to Kurdish. What makes the converting of the city into a Kurdish one right, when everyone, including the Kurds, strongly condemned Saddam Hussein's attempts at its Arabisation?

Furthermore, the Kurdish party leaders do not hesitate to declare publicly that Kirkuk is the "Kurdish Jerusalem." Given its oil wealth, they also hope it will be the mainstay of the future Kurdish economy. In order to strengthen their claims, Kurds—most of whom have never lived in Kirkuk—are moving to the city. Administration in Kirkuk today is largely in the hands of Kurds, and the city is subject to the rush of outsider Kurds in large numbers. For its part, the Kurdish leadership clearly intends for Kirkuk, rather than Arbil, to be the capital of their zone.

Canadian journalist Scott Taylor, a disinterested observer of the Turcoman-Kurdish animosities, described the circumstances bluntly: "With the great effort taken by the *peshmerga* to eradicate all registration and land deeds, a sinister programme of ethnic cleansing is underway." And he revealingly went on, "If *peshmerga* can flood the area with enough Kurdish settlers prior to a census then they will be able to substantiate their claims that Kirkuk is a Kurdish city. At the same time, because the Kurds control the borders, they are preventing Turcoman exiles from returning home."[59] It appears that

Taylor has a deeply intuitive understanding of Iraq. Policy makers would be well advised to heed these words of warning.

There are reports of the continuing displacement of Arabs from Kirkuk, many of whom are living around old military bases ten kilometres north of the city, according to local aid agencies. Others have taken refuge in abandoned schools inside Kirkuk or in small villages after being forced out by the Kurds. Many displaced Arabs are also living north of Baghdad in abandoned army camps and public buildings, most without access to health services, electricity, or running water.

According to Dexter Filkins, of the important mass-circulation American daily, *International Herald Tribune*, thousands of Kurds are pushing into lands formerly held by Arabs, forcing tens of thousands of them to flee to ramshackle refugee camps and transforming the demographical and political map of northern Iraq. He avers that the new movement, which began with the fall of Saddam Hussein, appears to have quickened in the spring of 2004, amid confusion about United States policy along with political pressure by Kurdish leaders to resettle the areas formerly held by Arabs. It is happening at a time when Kurdish officials are threatening to pull out of the national government if they cannot maintain enough autonomy. The perceptive American journalist emphasises that the biggest flashpoint is Kirkuk, a city contested by Kurds, Arabs, and Turcomans. Kurdish leaders want to make the city the Kurdish regional capital and resettle it with Kurds. To make the point, Filkins continues, some ten thousand Kurds have gathered in a sprawling camp outside Kirkuk, where they are pressing the United States to let them enter the city.[60]

The New York-based organisation Human Rights Watch, an independent group, warned on August 3, 2004, that tension over unresolved competing property and land claims in northern Iraq may soon explode into "open violence" between returning Kurds and Arab settlers. According to the report more than six thousand land claims are lodged at Iraqi Property and Claims Commission offices, which were set up in January 2004 by the Coalition Provisional Authority and are now run by the Iraqi government. It is said that unless the government acts to resolve the disputes, the region could be overwhelmed by a crisis of potentially "massive" proportions. The report urged the authorities to "address the immediate humanitarian needs of the thousands of internally displaced Kurds and other non-Arabs in and around the contested oil-rich city of Kirkuk." Over a thirty-year period, Saddam Hussein destroyed Kirkuk's ethnic balance to ensure the dominance of Arabs and to consolidate control over the region's oil fields. It is contended that as many as two hundred fifty thousand Kurds and Turcomans were expelled from their homes, including an estimated one hundred twenty thousand during the 1990s. But since the Baathi regime's collapse, some of those who were expelled have returned, demanding the restitution of property given to Arab settlers. Many live in dire conditions—camping in makeshift tents, abandoned factories, and the city's football stadium—as they await the resolution of their property claims.[61]

The Associated Press reported that as many as five hundred Kurds a day streamed into Kirkuk in August 2004, and United States officials agreed that the surge was timed to establish residency ahead of a census to be held in preparation for the elections. American military authorities, which control security in Kirkuk, were quoted by the Associated Press as saying that some seventy-two thousand refugees, mainly Kurds, had arrived in and around the city since April 2003, and about twenty thousand Kurds arrived in August 2004 alone, encouraged by Kurdish political parties, which gave them money or building supplies to help them reclaim their land. If they keep coming, the city of seven hundred fifty thousand could have one hundred thousand new residents before the first elections since Saddam Hussein was ousted in 2003. "Kirkuk is the key to avoiding civil war in Iraq," said the American officials. "Kirkuk is to Iraq what Kosovo is to the Balkans."[62]

At the turn of the year 2005, Richard Oppel Jr. of *International Herald Tribune* reported from Arbil that Kurdish residents in northern Iraq already called the area Kurdistan. In many places it was impossible to find an Iraqi flag. But the Kurds' red, white, and green standard, with a shining sun in the middle, flew everywhere, even atop an Iraqi border guard compound in far northeastern Iraq. The Kurdistan Democratic Party's minister of *peshmerga* affairs was quoted as saying, "We are ready to fight against all forces to control Kirkuk. Our share is very little. We will try to take a larger share."[63] On February 2, 2005, Peter Galbraith wrote in the same newspaper that the Kurdish region functioned as if it were an independent state. The Kurdistan Regional Government at Arbil carried out virtually all government functions, and Baghdad law applied only to the extent that the Kurdish parliament chose to apply it. The area was responsible for its own security and maintained its own armed forces. The Kurds did not allow Arab units of the new Iraqi military into their territory; nor did they permit Baghdad ministries to open offices. They refused to surrender control of their international borders to Baghdad for fear that the central government would cut off their access to the outside world.[64]

The city of Kirkuk and its environs has been in existence for a long time. The foundation of Turcoman Kirkuk belongs to the post-Abbasid period. It was a fine city by the sixteenth century. Its history had been that of a trading town and of a garrison city, from which sallies were undertaken into the mountains to the east. According to the first Ottoman-Iranian truce at Amasya on May 29, 1555, the territory became a part of the Ottoman dominions and resumed its former role as that of an important bulwark against an enemy from the east. Its position as an administrative centre has varied through the centuries. In the eighteenth century, Kirkuk was the headquarters of the Ottoman province of Şehrizor, comprising the districts of Kirkuk, Arbil, and Sulaimaniya. With the reforms of Mithat Paşa, the illustrious governor of Baghdad from 1869 to 1872 and a public servant of great ability, the name Şehrizor was given to the sanjak[65] of Kirkuk (corresponding to the present districts of Kirkuk and Arbil), while the historical Şehrizor remained outside, in the new sanjak of Sulaimaniya.[66]

The Mosul province was founded in 1879. Under the Ottomans this province was a land bridge on the trade routes that crossed Anatolia towards the Persian Gulf, and those which continued directly east on the Silk Road into Iran and central Asia. Sitting on the Tigris River and roughly equidistant from Aleppo, Diyarbekir, Tabriz, Hamadan, and Baghdad, Mosul was a focal point for military campaigns and commerce alike. It was a city situated at the centre of a regional economic network that extended into what today are Syria, Turkey, Iran, and Saudi Arabia. Kirkuk remained an important garrison town and, for reasons of language and the racial composition of the population, a valuable recruiting centre for civil servants and gendarmes on whom the Ottoman administration could rely. The Turcomans of Kirkuk had always provided strong support for the Ottoman Empire and its culture and were an abundant source of Ottoman officials.[67]

Kirkuk had just been occupied by British troops when the armistice of October 30, 1918, was concluded between the Ottoman Empire and the Allied powers. It must be specifically recorded here that because the majority of Kirkuk's population was Turkish, the Ottoman government had been unwilling to give up the area following the First World War. Based on Article 12 of the American President Woodrow Wilson's fourteen-point "Programme of the World's Peace"—unveiled on January 8, 1918, which stipulated that the Turkish portions of the Ottoman Empire should be assured a secure sovereignty—the Ottoman delegation to the Paris Peace Conference, in the memorandum of June 23, 1919, concerning the new organisation of the Ottoman Empire delivered to the Council of the Principal Allied and Associated Powers, stated the following: "In Asia the Turkish lands are bounded on the south by the provinces of Mosul and Diyarbekir, as well as a part of Aleppo as far as the Mediterranean."[68]

The Ottoman government's view was based mainly on the notions of nationality and self-determination, which had been increasingly popular as principles of political settlement, especially after the First World War. The right to self-determination that Wilson was granting to the peoples of Europe—the Czechs, Poles, and others—applied to Turks as well. They too had the right to a sovereign nation of their own.

Oil had been discovered around Kirkuk, thus strengthening Britain's desire to incorporate the province of Mosul into a new Iraqi state over which it could exercise control. Ankara, on the other hand, was determined that the aforesaid province should become part of Turkey. The Sivas Congress of September 4-11, 1919, laid down the principles that would become the National Pact[69] on January 28, 1920, which the Turkish national movement stated was the legitimate expression of the popular will and its minimum desiderata. This document explicitly renounced all Turkish demands over portions of the Ottoman Empire inhabited by an Arab majority but stated that all territories, within or outside armistice line—inhabited by a non-Arab Ottoman Moslem majority—could, under no juridical or equitable grounds, be separated from the new Turkey. Mesopotamia, Syria, Palestine, Arabia, and Egypt were the territories inhabited by an Arab majority; while a non-Arab Ottoman Moslem majority existed in the province of Mosul held by the British and the province of Adana and district of İskenderun held by the French.

Turkey even proposed that a plebiscite be held to establish the wishes of Mosul's population, which the British refused. Iraq was an imperial creation—designed to accommodate the political and economic needs of its creators rather than the desires of its citizens. According to the British, the real desires of the people of the province were not only hard to ascertain but were liable at any time to sudden change. The townsman might well prefer an administration, the country folk another. Local feuds, personal ambitions, irrelevant hopes or fears, and all sorts of accidental circumstances were likely to determine the sentiments of the moment. A plebiscite, the British alleged, could hardly be carried out in such a way as to have much moral value. In actual fact, however, the British government did not favour the project of plebiscite because it was fully aware of the situation that the majority of the province's inhabitants were Turkish feeling; and, in addition to this, it calculated that a considerable part of the non-Turkish population would prefer the state of Turkish citizenship to that of Iraqi nationality. The Turkish government felt so sure of the result that it had expressed its willingness to abide by the consequences of a fair plebiscite.[70]

Kirkuk remained under British rule and in 1921 passed under the rule of the government of the kingdom of Iraq. It was not until 1926 that it was definitely incorporated in this kingdom, after an agreement between Turkey and Britain regarding the fate of the province of Mosul. In accordance with the tripartite treaty signed between Turkey, Britain, and Iraq in Ankara on June 5, 1926, Mosul was given to Iraq. In exchange, for a period of twenty-five years, Iraq was to pay Turkey 10 percent of all royalties that it received from the Turkish Petroleum Company (to be called Iraqi Petroleum Company in 1929).[71] Significantly enough, according to unpublished sources at the British Foreign Office, Foreign Secretary Austen Chamberlain informed his ambassador in Ankara, Ronald Lindsay, on May 17, 1926, that the latter was at liberty to accept up to 20 percent for twenty-five years or, as Iraq would prefer, up to a maximum of 15 percent for seventy-five years of Turkey's participation in oil royalties. The British ambassador was instructed to negotiate with the Turkish minister of foreign affairs Tevfik Rüştü with a view to settlement on this basis.[72]

The 10 percent of Iraq's royalties assigned to Turkey for twenty-five years related not only to oil but to oil by-products and natural gas as well.[73] Many British Foreign and Colonial Office documents confirm this.[74] As part of the 1926 treaty, Turkey was given the option, within twelve months from the enforcement of the treaty, of capitalising the said royalties at 500,000 sterling, to be payable by Iraq at thirty days' notice. Turkey did not use this proposed option and preferred the option of payment of 10 percent of all royalties accruing to Iraq for twenty-five years. Amazingly, certain Turkish and Western historians contend that Turkey, starved as it was of resources to cover current expenditure, subsequently commuted its 10 percent share in the oil fields into a single lump sum cash payment.[75] This is simply not correct. Unquestionably, Iraq made the royalty percentage payments for the first twenty years; the necessary payment for the remaining five years has not been effected to date.[76]

The leading notable families of Kirkuk were Turcomans. The most important of these families were the Neftçis, who, as their name implies, owned and exploited the ancient oil seepages; the Yakuboğlus, landowners; and the Kırdars, who were both landowners and merchants. The Avcıs had spent a large fortune making an irrigation canal on their land in the Hawija plain bordering the Little Zab River. They were great sportsmen and fully upheld the family name, which in Turkish means "hunter." All four families were solid Turkish stock, and after the First World War their existence was a stabilising factor in local government.

It should be remembered that oil had a certain importance in Ottoman times, being used by the army. The springs were owned by the government, and were leased to contractors. The oil was collected in skins from pits and was carried by pack animals to the refineries. There were stills at Kirkuk, Tazehurmatu, and Mandali. The refined oil was used, according to quality, for illumination, lubrication, or as a specific for monge. An imperial decree of 1639 had recognised the monopoly of rights over the area's oil to the Neftçis.

There were also several Turcoman soldiers and civil servants who, though not members of the old and wealthy families, had reached high office in the Ottoman service and had returned to their province after the dismemberment of the empire. The Turcomans participated in the cultural, economic, and political life of the area to the point where they predominated. Many of the Turcoman landholders, forming the elite, had served in the local Ottoman administration. They retained the position of social influence they enjoyed under Ottoman rule. They benefited from the prestige of the past and an indisputable moral authority. The social weight of the Turcomans, therefore, was out of proportion to their numbers. They had an important presence in Iraqi affairs, beyond that warranted by their size.

Following the First World War, Turkish was still being used in Kirkuk, not only for local purposes but also in communications with Baghdad because all the civil servants were local men, of whom there was no dearth in this cradle of Ottoman officials. Thus Longrigg, the British assistant political officer for Kirkuk, could understandably write in November 1918 that "in the society of Kirkuk the Turkish official holds a leading place. It was, in fact, a nursery of officials—a few Kurdish or Arab, a few Christians, but the bulk of the local Turcoman breed."[77] There was a Turkish newspaper published there, and an association of Turcoman writers was in existence. *Necme,* the only local newspaper published daily in Turkish, was read in Kirkuk, Kifri, Arbil, and Sulaimaniya and distributed to the notables and officials of the district. Its sources were local news and articles, Reuter telegrams, and official notices.[78]

It is to be emphasised that A. F. Miller, the British assistant administrative inspector at Kirkuk, who dealt with town affairs including the municipality, could speak only Turkish. He was a good Turkish scholar but never learnt any Arabic or Kurdish. Not surprisingly, therefore, at the first meeting of the Kirkuk Divisional Council held on November 20, 1919, draft rules of procedure had been printed in Turkish by the office of the British political officer, and each member was given a copy. The draft rules of procedure were then laid before the members and passed entirely.[79]

The first Iraqi cabinet formed by Naqib of Baghdad Sayid Abd al-Rahman al-Gaylani on October 25, 1920, included a retired Turcoman general from Kirkuk, İzzet Paşa, a person of exceptional competence, at the Ministry of Education and Health. The latter also acted as minister of public works in the second Iraqi cabinet constituted on January 29, 1921. However, in November 1921, just three months into Emir Faisal's rule, İzzet Paşa resigned from his post in protest at the manner in which the Turcomans were being discriminated against. Ironically, his resignation did nothing to bring about reform. This was the last time a Turcoman held such a high office in Iraq's government.

The British Special Air Service officer at Kirkuk correctly reported in 1925 that "Izzet Pasha's Diwankhaneh is a meeting place for all pro-Turks and disgruntled elements. A man of courage and integrity, he was a rallying point for pro-Turks during the visit of the League of Nations' commissioners in 1925."[80] Cecil John Edmonds who had been involved in shaping and presenting British policy towards Iraq described him as a former general with an ability to influence the public opinion.[81] This is confirmed by the highly regarded American historian and once senior United States diplomat in Baghdad Philip Willard Ireland: "Izzet Pasha, of Turkish descent and a native of Kirkuk, had held military rank under the Ottoman government and had a considerable reputation throughout Iraq."[82]

To the dismay and disappointment of the British, at the time of the referendum of July 1921, the people in the Kirkuk area who opposed Arab rule did not vote for inclusion in the kingdom of Iraq and rejected Emir Faisal as its king; and from that moment, Turkish activities developed in the region, supported by a Turkish committee founded at Kirkuk by the Neftçi family and other Turcomans. Representatives of Kirkuk did not attend the accession ceremonies of Emir Faisal as king of Iraq on August 23, 1921.[83] Small wonder, as Christopher Catherwood, author of *Winston's Folly*, argues, Iraq after all was a make-believe state, cobbled together by Whitehall from the three Ottoman provinces of Mosul, Baghdad, and Basra at a conference in Cairo chaired by Winston Churchill, British colonial secretary at the time.[84]

The British lacked detailed understanding of the various peoples they were trying to meld into this new state and were handicapped by strong cultural stereotypes. Effectively, Kirkuk's Turcoman population was culturally and economically driven to Turkey. Local Turcoman notables identified with the

Turks across the border.[85] In Kirkuk, it was the Turcomans whose political influence was the strongest. Despite the fact that they were a law-abiding community, they were also a liability to the British claim for the retention of the Mosul province, which was in dispute between the years 1918 and 1926. Although one could not blame them for not wanting to be separated from Anatolia, they amounted to an opponent's stronghold behind British lines, and as such, required delicate handling.[86] In the words of Arnold Wilson, the first British high commissioner of Iraq and a veteran of Arab affairs with a decade of service in the Persian Gulf to his credit, "Kirkuk had always been a stronghold of Turkish officialdom, and pro-Turkish views here were a disturbing element for the occupation forces."[87] Given Wilson's great influence in shaping British policy towards Mesopotamia in the wake of the First World War, this statement may help one to grasp more fully some of the constraints and complexities that operated upon policy makers in London and among British administrators on the spot.

A Turcoman subgovernor and powerful and highly placed Turcoman officials who had served the Ottomans were appointed in 1921 to top administrative posts in Kirkuk as part of the British government's attempt to persuade the city's notables to participate in the elections for the Constituent Assembly. The purpose of these elections was to formalise the Treaty of Alliance of 1922 with Britain and obtain support for the drafting of a constitution and the passing of the Electoral Act of 1923. These elections had been organised by the British in order to bestow legitimacy upon the new rulers. The rationale was that this legitimacy would spill over and legitimise their own presence in the country. The Kirkuklis made their participation in the electoral process conditional on four provisos: (1) noninterference of the government in the electoral procedures, (2) the preservation of the Turkish character in the district's administration, (3) the recognition of Turkish as the district's official language, and (4) the appointment of Kirkuklis in all cabinets to be formed in Baghdad thereafter.[88]

In a telegram in Turkish sent in July 1923, the prime minister, Abd al-Muhsin al-Sadun, confirmed the Council of Ministers' acceptance of conditions 2 and 3, asking the subgovernor to transmit the government's decisions to the provisional administrative council formed by Kirkukli notables. This was a de facto recognition of their authority and a promise to safeguard Kirkuk's distinct cultural identity. However, these rights were not sufficient to induce the notables to register for the elections, underlining their unwillingness to become Iraqis. They wished to preserve the district's cultural and administrative autonomy.[89]

The Turcomans stress that their community has historically been in the majority in Kirkuk. Enough contemporary evidence exists to make it indisputable that Kirkuk is indeed Turkish. The heart of the city is inhabited by the Turcomans. They occupy the hill, known as the citadel, and form an exclusive community which refuses to be assimilated. The Turcomans who have lived in the old city since Ottoman times represent the stable city-community; merchants and proprietors of all kinds are Turcomans. Most of the cemeteries in Kirkuk are Turcoman. Interestingly, the British vice-consul in Mosul, H. E. Wilkie Young reported in 1910, "The Moslem population of Kirkuk (40,000) and Talafar (10,000) are Turcomans and there are a good many of them in the villages round about Mosul, e.g., Nebi Yunus, Yarimja, Al-Kasr, etc. Their language is a dialect of Turkish. They are very independent. There are 7,000 houses in the town of Kirkuk and the population is not less than 40,000, of whom about 2,500 are Jews, and only 630 Christians. The rest are Moslems of Turcoman origin. The language of the place is consequently Turkish."[90] This can hardly be disputed. Wilkie Young, after prolonged contact with all the local groups, saw the situation of the Ottoman population in a realistic light. The British representative's penetrating despatch describes the area perfectly.

Gertrude Bell, who was the British assistant political officer in Basra between 1916 and 1919 and served as oriental secretary to the civil administrator and later high commissioner of Iraq from 1919 to 1926, recorded in 1921, despite her powerful anti-Turkish bias: "The inhabitants of Kirkuk are largely of Turkish blood, descendants of Turkish settlers dating from the time of Seljuks. At Talafar a large proportion of the population is Turcoman. They claim descent from 100,000 Turkish prisoners captured by Tamerlane and spared from death. Turkish place names are common in the vicinity."[91] On balance, Bell's remarks were accurate. She is not alone here. British historian David Oates concurs with her in the Turcoman dominance of Talafar.[92]

Italian anthropologist Nelida Fuccaro points out that Talafar is inhabited by Turcomans. She mentions that their leaders are city notables and powerful landowners but at the same time retain authority over the sedentary population which is organised along kin ties.[93] Just as important, as late as autumn 2004, the American press could still highlight the fact that the Turcomans dominated Talafar's population. Talafar is one town where the Turcomans are definitely in the majority. This is a clear Turcoman area.[94] More recently Jonathan Finer of the *Washington Post* reported from the spot on September 3, 2005, that as many as 75 percent of Talafar's residents were Turcomans and claimed that many of them held prominent positions in the society before the American invasion.[95]

No less an astute observer of affairs as William Rupert Hay—who was the British political officer for Mandali, Altın Köprü, Köysanjak, and Arbil between 1918 and 1920—likewise related in 1921: "Starting with the Nebi Yunus (the tomb of the Prophet Jonah) on the bank of the Tigris opposite Mosul, and running down through Arbil, Altın Köprü, Kirkuk, Kifri, and Kızıl Robat to Mandali, we find a line of towns with Turkish-speaking inhabitants. It is practically the same line which divides predominantly Kurdish from predominantly Arab territory. Kirkuk is the main centre of this Turkish population, and before the war possessed 30,000 inhabitants. Several villages in its vicinity are also Turkish-speaking, whereas the other towns are isolated communities surrounded by Kurds and Arabs. Large numbers of the middle-class Turks of Kirkuk and Arbil who possess some land, but wish to augment their incomes, learn to read and write, wear European clothes and undertake appointments in government service. Kirkuk and Arbil, especially the former, provided large numbers of officials to the Ottoman government."[96] Hay's comments are valuable because he was able to do research, or at least to observe and visit, in many Turcoman areas in Iraq.

The same British political officer submitted a monthly report in December 1920 on Arbil that also warrants a brief quote: "The population of the town of Arbil amounts to about 14,000. Of these the greater part retains the Turkish language. The Arbili Turcoman is remarkable for his vivacity and his polite manners. The leading people are unusually cultivated and are well acquainted with European politics. They show a real interest in all new inventions and are most urgent in demanding a sound modern education for their children. They are very free from religious prejudice, and Mulla Effendi, the leading divine, dines regularly in European style."[97] Hay, due to his knowledge of the real situation and sheer human compassion, could not help reporting to his government the true state of affairs.

According to Edmonds, whose appointment lasted two and a half years in the area, the population of Kirkuk in 1922 numbered around twenty-five thousand, of whom the great majority were Turcomans and about one-quarter Kurds, with smaller colonies of Arabs, Christians, and Jews. He also mentions that the leading families of Kifri considered themselves Turks; the population in general was mixed Turcoman and Kurdish.[98] Edmonds's knowledge of the local languages and his intimate acquaintance with the land and people of northeast Iraq helped him to be one of the best informed on the region. It should be remembered that he also served as a British liaison officer on the

League of Nations' Commission of Inquiry on the disputed area of Mosul between Turkey and Britain from 1924 to 1925.

The memorandum submitted by the British delegation during the Lausanne Peace Conference on December 14, 1922, admitted that the town of Talafar was an almost exclusively Turkish town and that there was a large group of Turkish villages round Mosul. It was, in fact, the case that the area of Sheikhan—which depended on Mosul and included sixty-eight villages—and that of Ashar Seba—which included seventy-eight—were populated entirely by Turks, and that the area which depended directly on Mosul and included seventy-seven villages, was populated by Turks in a great majority. The existence all around Mosul of villages bearing purely Turkish names such as Kara Koyunlu, Kara Ali, Keçi Hane, Narin Köprü, and Büyük Köşk was further proof of what has just been stated.[99] The Turkish character of this district and of the Kirkuk and Arbil areas was, moreover, recognised by the British government itself, since the proclamations addressed by British officials to the local population were drawn up in the same Turkish language as that in use in İstanbul.[100]

The Council of the League of Nations, during its thirtieth session at the meeting held in Geneva on September 30, 1924, which was devoted to the examination of the question of the frontiers of Iraq, decided to set up a special commission of three members, with a view to collecting the facts and data that it required to fulfil the mission entrusted to it under Article 3, paragraph 2, of the Lausanne Peace Treaty of July 24, 1923.[101] Kirkuk, as this commission of inquiry reported on July 16, 1925, was Turkish. "The leading men were Turkish and in their houses they spoke Turkish with the members of their families. Even the Christians of Kirkuk spoke Turkish among themselves."[102]

Arbil, the commission also wrote, was divided into seven boroughs. "We interviewed the *mukhtars* of these boroughs. When asked what was their nationality five replied that they were Turks, one that he was as much a Turk as a Kurd, and the seventh stated that he was a Jew." The commission spent some two months in the disputed area, visiting the principal localities, interrogating leading inhabitants and representatives of all classes and creeds. The commission, after their first experience in Mosul, decided to split into three—one member to each subdistrict, investigating all aspects of local life, the people's origins, religions, languages, cultivation, trade, transport, and finally, and in private, their wishes for future government—Turkish and Iraqi. On completion of their individual studies, they would re-form, study each other's notes, and then revisit each subdistrict together for a final inquiry before returning to Switzerland to complete their report and recommendations. Language was not always reliable evidence of political views. Many Arabic speakers, particularly those of the poorer classes, were pro-Turkish and sometimes gave touching expressions to their sympathies. The authors of the report refuted the validity of the distinction that the British government had sought to make between the Turks and the Turcomans. They stated that the Turks in Mosul, whom the British foreign secretary, Lord Curzon, called Turcomans, as distinct from Turks, were truly Turks.[103]

The commission, which examined the problem on the spot, further noted, "The towns and villages along the old trade route that led from Anatolia along the foothills of the Zagros to Baghdad are mainly Turkish speaking, being Turcoman. The town of Altın Köprü is definitely Turkish. The population of Tuzhurmatu is, except a few Jewish families, entirely Turkish. Thirty-five out of 405 families of the town are Jewish. The population of Kara Tepe is seventy-five percent Turk, twenty-two percent Kurd, and three percent Arab. Tazehurmatu and Daquq are also mainly Turkish."[104]

It is also relevant to quote Hanna Batatu, the well-known American specialist on Iraqi history and politics, who draws attention to the fact that "Kirkuk had been Turkish through and through in the not too distant past." Batatu is particularly subtle in his ambitious treatment of the relationship between ethnic, regional, and economic factors; and he elaborates, "By degrees, Kurds moved into the city from the surrounding villages. With the growth of the oil industry, their migration intensified. By 1959, they had swollen to more than one-third of the population; and the Turcomans had declined to just over half, the Assyrians and Arabs accounting, in the main, for the rest of the total of one hundred twenty thousand. Other Turkish towns, such as Arbil, had undergone a similar process: Arbil itself was in great measure Kurdified, and the change occurred peacefully. But the Kirkuklis, who maintained close cultural links with Turkey, were of a tougher fibre and united by a stronger sense of ethnic identity."[105]

This influx of Kurds into heavily Turcoman-populated areas impaired the fragile demographic balance and laid the groundwork for decades of ethnic tension. Inevitably, antagonism began to develop between the original Turcoman population of Kirkuk and the more recent Kurdish incomers. By the end of 1958, a number of sensitive appointments in the city were given to the Kurds, with the result that the Turcomans, who had always dominated the socioeconomic and political life of the city, felt themselves increasingly at a disadvantage. There was serious and substantive cause for concern.[106] The worst episode came in 1959 when, instigated by the Iraqi

Communist Party, a group largely comprising Kurds went on a rampage against the city's more prosperous Turcomans, leading to a three-day massacre of Kirkuk's Turcoman leaders that only stopped when Baghdad intervened militarily.[107]

CHAPTER III

THE INTERNATIONAL LEGAL
RIGHTS OF THE TURCOMANS

THE ANGLO-IRAQI TREATY of Alliance of June 30, 1930, signifying the end of the British mandate in 1932, failed to specify minority rights.[108] In this treaty Britain did not press for the inclusion of safeguards for the minority communities. If such safeguards were necessary, the British government thought that it was the responsibility of the League of Nations to insist upon them, while considering the question of the termination of the mandate and the admission of Iraq into the League. Such a procedure would not be unusual since on several occasions in the past the League had required applicants for membership in the organisation to give pledges regarding the good treatment of minorities. The League accepted this view. The emphasis which it placed on the giving of guarantees by Iraq regarding minorities, however, indicated the seriousness with which it regarded the question.[109]

On September 4, 1931, the Council of the League of Nations requested the Permanent Mandates Commission to submit its opinion on the proposal of the British government for the emancipation of Iraq. The task entrusted by the council to the commission consisted of giving opinion as to whether, in the case of Iraq, the time for putting an end to the mandatory regime—a regime which, from its inception, had possessed certain special features—had arrived; and defining the guarantees that would, in that case, be given by Iraq to the League of Nations. The commission pointed out that the question as to whether a people, which had hitherto been under the mandatory regime, had become fit to stand alone was above all a question of fact. In determining their ability to do so, it was necessary not only to ascertain whether the country—which was desirous of emancipation—had at the present time the essential political institutions and administrative machinery of a modern state, but also whether it showed evidence of such social conditions and civic spirit as would be required to ensure the regular working of these institutions and the effective exercise of civil and political rights as established by law.[110]

The Permanent Mandates Commission expressed that it had no opportunity to observe firsthand the moral condition and internal policy of Iraq, the degree of efficiency reached by its administrative organisation, and the spirit in which its laws were applied and in which its institutions functioned. In judging the actual situation in Iraq, the commission could therefore only endeavour to reach a conclusion on the basis of the annual reports of the mandatory power and the special report entitled "Progress of Iraq during the Period 1920-1931," together with the explanations furnished year by year by the accredited representatives of the mandatory power during the examination of these reports and the numerous petitions addressed to the League of Nations by inhabitants or by third parties with the observations of the mandatory power upon them. The views of the British government as to the political maturity of Iraq were the views of the guide who had constantly seen and directed the rapid progress made by that country during the mandatory regime.[111]

Some members of the Permanent Mandates Commission, and especially its Belgian representative and rapporteur, Pierre Orts, former secretary-general of the Ministry of Foreign Affairs, was not convinced that the guarantees laid down in the Iraqi Constitution adequately safeguarded the future of racial and religious minorities. The mandates section of the League of Nations Secretariat had exhaustively collected material about the mandates. The commission, the majority of whose members were natives of nonmandatory states, received information from various sources. In addition to that provided in the reports of the mandatory power and the replies of the accredited representatives, there were the petitions and information from other private sources. The commission had received information to the effect that Article 6 of the Iraqi Constitution, which provided that all Iraqis were equal before the law, would be a dead letter, and the protection of minorities therefore illusory.[112]

The Permanent Mandates Commission was concerned about the future security of minority communities; and in its report of November 13, 1931, in a rare exercise of its limited rights, expressed the opinion that as part of the conditions of its emancipation from the mandatory regime and in addition to satisfying certain tests of its capacity for full self-governance, Iraq must also be prepared to offer to the League of Nations guarantees on certain matters of international concern. In accord with the recommendations of the commission, the League Council appointed a special committee to draft a formal declaration of guarantees. Of these guarantees, those to which the commission had directed its principal attention were the protection of minorities, the judicial rights of foreigners, and the concession of the most-favoured-nation treatment to states members of the League, which is subject to reciprocity.[113]

When Iraq's application for admission to the League of Nations came up for consideration in 1932, the Council of the League required and received from the Iraqi government a written declaration defining the areas where the minority languages, local administration, law courts, and primary education were to function. This declaration of May 30, 1932, was to rank as part of the constitution, reaffirming Iraq's undertakings in regard to minorities. The mechanism was certification that Iraq, as the first Arab state to be admitted to the League, had been prepared for and was ready to assume its place among modern nations, capable of governing itself in accordance with the standards of the Geneva institution.[114]

Of the sixteen articles in the declaration assented to by the Iraqi government, ten deal with the protection of minorities. These articles—which were drafted in consultation with Nuri Said, the Iraqi premier—are based on the terms of a similar declaration that Albania was required to give before it was admitted to the League of Nations, but include some additional guarantees. In making public the text of the articles, the League expressed satisfaction that many of the "constitutional and legal provisions of Iraq are based on a very liberal conception of the rights to be accorded to racial, linguistic and religious minorities."[115]

Under Article 1 the stipulations contained in the declaration were recognised as fundamental laws of Iraq; and no law, regulation, or official action should conflict or interfere with these stipulations; nor should any law, regulation, or official action, then or in the future, prevail over them. In conformity with Article 4, notwithstanding the establishment by the Iraqi government of Arabic as the official language and notwithstanding the special arrangements to be made by the Iraqi government—under Article 9 of the present declaration—regarding the use of the Kurdish and Turkish languages, adequate facilities would be given to all Iraqi nationals whose mother tongue was not the official language for the use of their language—either orally or in writing—before the courts.

Article 8 stated that in the public educational system in towns and districts in which were residents a considerable proportion of Iraqi nationals whose mother tongue was not the official language, the Iraqi government would make provision for adequate facilities for ensuring that in the primary schools instruction should be given to the children of such nationals through the medium of their own language.

According to Article 9, Iraq pledged that in the districts of Mosul, Arbil, Kirkuk, and Sulaimaniya and in the subdistricts in which the population was predominantly of Kurdish race, the official language, side by side with Arabic, should be Kurdish. In the subdistricts of Kirkuk and Kifri, where a considerable part of the population was of Turcoman race, the official language, side by side with Arabic, should be either Kurdish or Turkish. Iraq undertook that in the said subdistricts officials should, although subject to justifiable exceptions, have a competent knowledge of Kurdish or Turkish as the case may be. Although in these subdistricts the criteria for the choice of officials would be, as in the rest of Iraq, efficiency and knowledge of the language, rather than race, Iraq undertook that the officials should, as hitherto, be selected, so far as possible, from among Iraqis from one or other of these subdistricts.

In accordance with Article 10, the stipulations of this declaration—so far as they affected persons belonging to linguistic or religious minorities—were declared to constitute obligations of international concern and would be placed under the guarantee of the League of Nations. No modifications could be made in them without the assent of a majority of the Council of the League of Nations. Any member of the League represented on the council should have the right to bring to the attention of the council any infraction or danger of infraction of any of these stipulations, and the council might thereupon take such measures and give such directions as it may deem proper and effective in the circumstances. Any difference of opinion as to questions of law or fact arising out of these articles between Iraq and any member of the League of Nations represented on the council should be held to be a dispute of an international character under Article 14 of the Covenant of the League of Nations. Any such dispute should, if the other party thereto demanded, be referred to the Permanent Court of International Justice. The decision of the Permanent Court should be final and should have the same force and effect as an award under Article 13 of the Covenant.

It is of great importance to note that this Iraqi declaration to the League of Nations recognised Kirkuk and Kifri as predominantly Turcoman. Turkish was mentioned as one of the official languages of these districts. Equal minority rights were granted to the Kurds and the Turcomans alike. Most writers on Iraq in this period seem to have overlooked this crucial point. As cited in the preceding paragraphs, the declaration includes a number of international obligations and sets out guarantees for the rights of the Turcomans that Iraq is not allowed to amend or abolish. Most fundamentally, Iraq, in 1932, recognised for the first time the Turcomans as an officially constituted ethnic minority with legal rights—a condition, determined by the League of Nations, for gaining independence.

Iraq became a member of the United Nations on December 21, 1945, while it was still a member of the then existing League of Nations and without having then or since sought, obtained, or effected any reduction in the formal international obligations it incurred voluntarily and laid out bindingly in the 1932 declaration. Resolutions passed at the end of the twenty-first and last formal meeting of the League of Nations Assembly on April 18, 1946, in Geneva reaffirmed those guarantees upon which Iraq's independence and territorial integrity depended. These obligations have been transferred to the United Nations and are still in effect to this day.[116]

But even before this, the Iraqi government—aware of the apprehensions expressed by the League of Nations, the European press, and the Parliament at Westminster—had set about reassuring them by the enactment of some laws for the benefit of minorities. For linguistic minorities, the Local Languages Law No. 74 of 1931 provided that the official language should be Kurdish or Turkish in a number of the northern districts and, in addition, that in all primary schools in these districts the language of instruction should be that of the majority of pupils. The law accepted Kirkuk and Kifri as areas inhabited by Turcoman majorities.[117]

CHAPTER IV

TURCOMAN APPREHENSION

KIRKUK IS AN urban centre with a strong Ottoman flavour, and its Turkish quality has never been in question. No traveller, proceeding from the south, can fail to be struck, when he reaches Kirkuk, by the fact that he has passed into an area of different culture. Kirkuk resembles the Turkish towns of Anatolia rather than those of Arabia. In terms of its inhabitants, architecture, language, and customs, Kirkuk is a truly Turkish city, bearing a closer appearance to Bursa than Baghdad.[118] Hence, it is no wonder that Reader Bullard, of the British Levant Consular Service, who served as political officer in Kifri and Mosul between 1918 and 1920 and later acted as military governor of Baghdad in 1920, maintains the idea in 1961 that "the largest of the Turkish towns in Iraq is Kirkuk."[119] It is worthwhile to recall that Bullard knew that particular region well, for he attended the first part of the Lausanne Peace Conference from November 20, 1922 to February 4, 1923, to deal with the fate of the Mosul province; and much earlier, in a diary entry dated May 20, 1918, this expert administrator had already noted thus: "I am appointed Political Officer, Kirkuk. At present I am running Kifri too. Kirkuk town alone has about thirty thousand inhabitants. The town people are Turks, and Turkish is the common language. Turkish is spoken in most places."[120]

"Kirkuk is mainly Turcoman," reported Julian Borger, as late as 2002 from Washington DC, for his prestigious British daily the *Guardian*.[121] Borger was certainly right. Kirkuk still remained a city of Turcoman character despite efforts to the contrary.

Kirkuk has become one of the most divisive political issues in Iraq. The Iraqi government and the Kurds have never been able to agree on whether or not Kirkuk should be included in a Kurdish region. This is of particular historical importance since it was at the root of the collapse of the 1970 autonomy agreement between the Kurds and the central government in Baghdad. The Kurds consider the oil fields of Kirkuk to be theirs. They are not. They are part of the national patrimony. Naturally, no Iraqi government would be prepared to surrender control of the country's most vital resource. The oil and other natural resources of Iraq are for the Iraqi people. That is to whom they belong, and that is whom they should benefit. Iraq's vast oil wealth is an asset of inestimable potential and must be developed for the future good of all the country's citizens. There can be no question about oil in the north being solely for the profit of Kurds.

The Iraqi National Oil Company has been reconstituted, and there is every indication that the revenues will flow directly into the centre, to be distributed elsewhere. Oil is an asset that should give benefit to Iraqis equally. Major oil proposals need to be well prepared by groups of experts, deliberated upon extensively, and approved by a legitimate authority. However, Kurdish groups have preempted this process and started signing deals and memoranda of understanding with minor energy firms. The Iraqi Ministry of Oil has threatened to blackball these firms. The Kurds are keen to include Kirkuk in their region, since they believe that if it is included, their demands on the national oil revenue would be justified.

Iraqi Kurdish leaders have called on the United States to support their plans "to own and manage Kurdistan's natural resources, and in particular our efforts to develop new oil resources in the Kurdistan region, where the previous regime sought to block all exploration and development that might benefit the Kurdish people." The demand was one of many set out in a letter by Massoud Barzani and Jalal Talabani, leaders of the Kurdistan Democratic Party and the Patriotic Union of Kurdistan, respectively, and sent to President George Bush on June 1, 2004. The Kurds' demand to develop northern reserves runs counter to the vision of a centralised oil industry set out by the coalition authorities and the Iraqi oil sector itself. Article 25, clause E of the transitional administrative law of March 8, 2004, states that "management of Iraq's natural resources, which are owned by the people of Iraq, will be conducted in consultation with regions and governorates, with the distribution of revenue through the public budget made in an equitable manner in accordance with demographic distribution in various areas of the country taking into account those areas that were unfairly denied access to revenue by the previous regime, as well as the need and level of development in various regions of the country."[122]

The prime minister of the Kurdistan Regional Government at Arbil, Nechirvan Barzani, reiterated on June 25, 2004, in a *Reuters* interview the prevailing view among Kurds that Kirkuk should be returned to their control. While prepared to negotiate with Baghdad over the sharing of all revenues from existing oil fields in the Kirkuk area, Barzani insisted that "all income from future oil finds there should belong to the Kurds themselves." Regarding possible oil development in northern Iraq, Norway's DNO ASA announced on June 30, 2004, that it had entered into an agreement with the Kurdistan Regional Government "to explore for and develop oil and gas in the region. DNO will be the operator and sole contractor for the area covered by the agreement." The statement gave no details of the area in question or any other aspects of the deal. But it added that the Norwegian company was "very pleased with this new and encouraging opportunity with the Kurdistan Regional Government to exploit hydrocarbon resources in northern Iraq."[123]

For political and military reasons there has been no exploration undertaken in northern Iraq for hydrocarbon reserves over the past half century. Whether any future operations are undertaken at the direction of the Kurdistan Regional Government or the central government in Baghdad depends on the shape of the new Iraq that will emerge in the future. DNO appears to concede this element of doubt when it says that while the "Kurdistan Regional Government has controlled its natural resources since 1991, future legal and constitutional developments in Iraq could affect operations under this agreement." Farther in the past, a model production-sharing agreement drafted in 2002 by the Interim Joint Regional Government of North Iraq, the Sulaimaniya Regional Government, and the Turkish electric power company General Elektrik, sets out terms and conditions under which an international contractor would be able to undertake oil and gas development work in northern Iraq. Australian Global Petroleum announced in November 2003 that it had formed a joint venture with Fira International to apply for the Chamchamal area in northern Iraq and to undertake petroleum operations in the region. The outcome of the application is awaited.[124]

Against this background, the Iraqi Ministry of Oil has warned international oil companies against entering into negotiations on future oil development with any party other than the country's central government. The warning came in a press statement released on July 16, 2004, outlining the government's policy for the development of natural resources in Iraq. Due to its importance, the summary text of the statement of the Ministry of Oil is given as follows: "Ownership of Iraq's natural resources, including oil and natural gas, rests with the entire Iraqi people. The authority to exploit or take new decisions relating to the exploration, development, production and handling of oil and natural gas has been and will remain a sovereign right of the central government of Iraq, and such decisions will be made on the basis of Iraqi national laws. Oil and natural gas resources will be developed by our national oil companies in consultation with the provinces and governorates of Iraq, whether directly by national efforts or in cooperation with highly qualified international oil companies. Such development shall be in accordance with open and transparent bidding processes and internationally recognised business codes of conduct. As part of this policy companies that wish to be welcomed here in the future should not enter into or try to pursue the implementation of agreements with persons who are not empowered to represent the sovereign government of Iraq. The respect of Iraqi law and relevant international laws by the companies in the past will be taken into consideration in negotiations for future agreements with the sovereign government of Iraq."[125]

On December 29, 2004, Iraq's Oil Ministry awarded its first contract since the fall of the Baathi regime, choosing three companies—Turkish, British, and local—to develop a northern oil field. The joint venture was awarded a 136-million-dollar deal to develop the Khurmala dome in the northern province of Arbil. The new oil field would have a capacity of 100,000 barrels a day and about 100 million cubic metres of associated gas. The Iraqi company Kar would work with Turkey's Avrasya and British-based Dynamic Processing Solutions in developing the field. Oil officials in Baghdad said more contracts with other companies would soon follow. The agreement came with Iraq's vital oil industry still in turmoil, with pipelines and other infrastructure frequently targeted by insurgents. On December 27 the ministry announced it would open bidding for a new contract to protect pipelines.[126]

There are steps being taken in the north that are challenging the traditionally centralised structure of the Iraqi oil industry. According to the Kurdistan Democratic Party satellite television on September 29, 2004, as reported by the British Broadcasting Corporation, a national oil corporation with wide authority has been established by Massoud Barzani's Kurdistan Democratic Party. According to the report, "the Kurdistan National Assembly, the parliament, concluded the proceedings of its eighty-fourth session in the transitional phase, which included four items. The items comprised the endorsement of a law on the Public Corporation for Oil, Gas and Petrochemicals in the Iraqi Kurdistan region, which included eleven clauses stipulating that the corporation is to be linked to the chairman of the Council of Ministers, to be managed by experts in the fields that concern the corporation, and the corporation is to have its own independent budget. The corporation is to be established with a view to attracting local and foreign companies and institutions and encouraging them to invest in the exploration of oil and gas fields, transport and refine oil and natural gas, transport, distribute and market oil and gas products, and develop the oil services sector."[127]

Canada's Heritage Oil announced on December 13, 2004, that it had formed a joint venture with the Eagle Group of Iraq in Iraqi Kurdistan, becoming the third international firm to make such a move. A statement said Heritage and Eagle had incorporated a jointly owned company, Heritage Erbil Oil Limited, with an authorised capital of twenty-five million dollars. Heritage Erbil has in turn incorporated K Petroleum Company, a wholly owned subsidiary of Heritage registered in both Baghdad and Arbil. Heritage and Eagle Group will each hold a 42.5 percent stake in K Petroleum Company, while Turkish investors will own the remaining 15 percent. The Heritage statement said that K Petroleum Company would be "working in close collaboration with the Iraqi Ministry of Oil. The company has been incorporated with the knowledge and support of the ministry. Discussions have already commenced. It is anticipated during this interim period, when there is an absence of hydrocarbon legislation in the country, that the license might initially be a service agreement, with a view to converting this into a production-sharing contract." The company said it would target "significant proven reserves with a plan to produce over 50,000 barrels per day, while assessing further known potential reserves in the region," and survey unexplored areas.[128]

Prime Minister Barzani confirmed that the new joint venture would operate "within a framework of a close working relationship with our regional government and the Ministry of Oil in Baghdad, utilising available local resources. The company should be in a position to commence its activities immediately in view of the stability prevailing in the region, which is far more stable than other parts of Iraq." Whether or not the new venture can maintain harmony with Baghdad in the event of new commercial discoveries of oil being made remains to be seen. Iraq's abundant oil wealth is likely to lead to intense competition over the distribution of profits.[129]

With the legal and regulatory environment as yet uncertain, the beginning of serious negotiations to develop Iraq's giant new fields is not anticipated in the near future. The Iraqi Oil Ministry is likely to focus instead on technical service agreements aimed at rehabilitating and enhancing existing production which is showing clear signs of duress in both the northern and southern fields.

The rights of the Turcomans who live among the Kurds must be protected from both central and regional governments. Thus far, the experience of the Turcomans under Kurdish rule has not been much different than their experience under the pervasive, coercive Baathi administration. Little has changed today. Violence is assuming a troubling pattern. Since April 10, 2003, Turcoman towns from Altın Köprü—including Kirkuk, Daquq, and

Tuzhurmatu—to Mandali have been occupied by Kurdish militants, who are constantly harassing Turcoman and Arab residents. Tensions flared between members of the Kurdish and Turcoman communities in Tuzhurmatu and Kirkuk in late August 2003. Some three days of clashes saw twelve people killed. At the heart of the tensions were disputes over political control of Tuzhurmatu. The arrival of the Kurdish militiamen was an attempt to grab power. The positions of mayor and police chief were given to Kurds. So were other powerful government posts.

More violence erupted in Kirkuk on December 31, 2003, when several thousand Turcomans and Arabs demonstrated outside the Patriotic Union of Kurdistan office in the city, shouting, "No to federalism, Kirkuk is Iraqi." Shooting broke out, killing five people and wounding some twenty others. Outbreaks of violence in the city continued into 2004 and 2005. Several leading Turcoman politicians have been assassinated. In May 2004, Ahmet Necmettin, one of the leaders of the Turcoman Union Party, was gunned down in Kirkuk just twelve days after Mustafa Kemal Yayçılı, a senior Iraqi Turcoman Front figure in the city, was also shot dead. Gunmen on June 3, 2005, killed Brigadier Sabah Karaaltın, a Turcoman official with the Kirkuk city council. Things in Kirkuk might well get out of hand, and the communities there find themselves in a violent standoff.

Officials from the Turcoman organisations in Kirkuk believe that the Kurds are trying to rewrite history. They say more than a hundred thousand of Kurds who were not originally from Kirkuk moved to the city to change its demographic balance ahead of the elections on January 30, 2005. They describe the city as the centre of the Turcoman people. In Kirkuk itself, Turcoman flags—a white crescent and several stars on a light blue background—cover virtually every available surface in their neighbourhoods of the city and are suspended from wires strung across many streets. The Iraqi flag, invisible in the rest of northern Iraq, is also widely displayed. The Turcomans want to see the creation of a government for a unified nation, the establishment of a democratic government where all the different people and parties in Iraq and all ethnic groups have a chance to be represented and get together and decide the government of the country. They prefer a federal Iraq based on geographic borders rather than ethnic groupings; but if the Kurds insist on an autonomous zone, they would demand an autonomous Turcoman one—with control of Kirkuk.

After Saddam Hussein's fall, the Patriotic Union of Kurdistan and Kurdistan Democratic Party seized control of key positions within Kirkuk's security forces, and the January 30, 2005 elections put Kurds in control of the provincial government. They have also emerged as the United States military's main ally in the fight against insurgents in the region, providing intelligence, support, and manpower. Most Turcomans are concerned that the Americans are being duped by the Kurds, whom they consider to be cloaking what is effectively a power grab and passing it off as a crackdown on the insurgents.

On June 15, 2005, Steve Fainaru and Anthony Shadid of the *Washington Post* reported from Kirkuk that police and security units, forces led by Kurdish political parties and backed by the United States military, have abducted hundreds of Arabs and Turcomans in this intensely volatile city and spirited them to prisons in Kurdish-led northern Iraq, as attested by United States and Iraqi officials, government documents, and families of the victims. Seized off the streets of Kirkuk or in joint American-Iraqi raids, the men have been transferred secretly and in violation of Iraqi law to prisons in the Kurdish cities of Arbil and Sulaimaniya, sometimes with the knowledge of United States forces. The detainees—including merchants, members of tribal families, and soldiers—have often remained missing for months; some have been tortured, according to released prisoners and the Kirkuk police chief. A confidential State Department cable—obtained by the *Washington Post* and addressed to the White House, the Pentagon, and the United States embassy in Baghdad—said the "extra-judicial detentions" were part of a "concerted and widespread initiative" by Kurdish political parties "to exercise authority in Kirkuk in an increasingly provocative manner." The abductions have "greatly exacerbated tensions along purely ethnic lines" and endangered United States credibility, the nine-page cable, dated June 5, 2005, stated. "Turcomans in Kirkuk tell us they perceive a United States tolerance for the practice, while Arabs in Kirkuk believe coalition forces are directly responsible."[130]

Some abductions occurred more than a year ago. But according to United States officials, Kirkuk police, and Arab leaders, the campaign surged after the January 30, 2005 elections consolidated control of the Patriotic Union of Kurdistan and the Kurdistan Democratic Party over the Kirkuk provincial government. The United States military stated it had logged 180 cases; Arab and Turcoman politicians put the number at more than 600 and said many families feared retribution for coming forward. United States and Iraqi officials, along with the State Department cable, considered the campaign as being orchestrated and carried out by the Kurdish intelligence agency known as Asayesh, and the Kurdish-led Emergency Services Unit, a five-hundred-member antiterrorism squad within the Kurdish police force. Both are closely allied with the United States military. The intelligence agency is made up of

Kurds, Arabs, and Turcomans. The cable indicated that the problem extended
to Mosul and regions near the Kurdish-controlled border with Turkey. The
transfers occurred "without authority of local courts or the knowledge of
Ministries of Interior or Defence in Baghdad," the State Department cable
stated. United States military officials said the judges they consulted in Kirkuk
declared the practice illegal under Iraqi law.[131]

General Turhan Yusuf Abdel-Rahman, the chief of Kirkuk's police force,
described the abductions as "political kidnappings" orchestrated by the
Kurdish parties and their intelligence arms. Abdel-Rahman, who is Turcoman
career officer, pointed out that his officers were taking part in the majority
of the abductions despite his attempts to stop the practice. He underlined
that 40 percent of Kirkuk's 6,210-member police force was loyal to the two
Kurdish political parties. Acting on the parties' orders, uniformed polices
carried out the abductions using the police department's cars and pickup
trucks, he continued. "The main problem is that the loyalty of the police is
to the parties and not the police force," added Abdel-Rahman. "They will
obey the parties' orders and disobey us." The head of the Emergency Services
Unit, Colonel Khattab Abdullah Arif, is a Patriotic Union of Kurdistan loyalist
and former Kurdish militia fighter with no previous police experience. The
provincial police director-general, Major General Sherko Shakir Hakim, most
recently worked as a taxi driver.[132]

For decades Kurds have complained of abuses against them, including
intimidation, expulsions, and property seizures. Now the Kurds are indulging
in some of Saddam Hussein's abuses themselves. The Turcomans say that
the Kurdish Regional Government is trying to increase its influence in the
same way Saddam Hussein's regime had been doing since the 1970s. The
intimidation appears widespread. As these unjust practices continue, the
Turcomans become more worried. Things can indeed get much worse for
them. Kurds must be persuaded to cease their violations of fundamental
human rights and to accept international verification of their human rights
practices.

Great apprehension is felt among the Turcomans. They are anxious about
their future. The massacre of the Turcomans by Kurds on July 14-16, 1959,
at Kirkuk should not be allowed to recur. Several scores of Turcomans lost
their lives in the ghastly slaughter. First reports gave the number of dead as
over one hundred, including women and children and large numbers seriously
wounded. Unsuspecting victims had been invited to come out of their houses,
and they had then been murdered and their mutilated bodies carried through
the streets of the city.

On these bloody incidents, the eminent British historian George Kirk, basing his description on eyewitness reports, convincingly wrote, and it is worth quoting him at length, "Approving Premier Abdul Karim Kassem's attempts to contain the communists, the Turcomans prepared to celebrate the first anniversary of the republican revolution by erecting 133 triumphal arches on the expanse of their community. Quarrels broke out between the Turcoman celebrators and the Kurdish communists. Fights at the city's bridge, in the two cinemas, and in one of its biggest cafés, ended with several persons wounded, and most of the Turcoman triumphal arches were burned. Then the communist-dominated People's Resistance Forces stormed the police station, looted the arms stored there, and drove the Turcomans into their homes. Troops of the Second Division, composed largely of Kurds, were sent to Kirkuk to restore order, but instead took the side of the Kurds. Some of its units shelled Turcoman houses and the troops were soon in command of the whole city. On 15 and 16 July, the Kurdish communists, with the help of the Second Division, ruled in Kirkuk. The mayor (a Kurdish communist) had ordered the executions of several groups of Turcoman notables and had them buried in mass graves outside the city. A few days later, Kassem gave out the number of dead as 120, the majority massacred by the Kurdish communists in conditions of great cruelty."[133]

On July 20, 1959, Humphrey Trevelyan, the British ambassador in Baghdad, wrote to his superiors in the Foreign Office that according to reports to the Turkish embassy by the Turks from Kirkuk who arrived in Baghdad, the troubles began in the evening of July 14, although preparations might have been made by the Kurds earlier. After a Turkish café was set on fire, a Kurdish mob, swelled by members of the People's Resistance Forces, attacked the houses of leading Turks, some of whom were killed. Kurdish troops of the Second Division joined in, and for the whole of July 15 the situation was out of hand. Some Turks took refuge in the citadel, from which dissident Kurdish troops tried to dislodge them with mortars. On July 16 order was restored by armoured and infantry units. Trevelyan stated that the Iraqi minister of foreign affairs, Hashim Jawad, a moderate in politics, told him that the troubles were started by deliberate communist provocation. Some of the troops had failed to act, and it had therefore been necessary to send troops to Kirkuk from outside.[134]

On July 24, 1959, Peter Hayman, the chargé d'affaires of the British embassy in Baghdad, in a letter to the Foreign Office, outlined the sequence of the Kirkuk massacre in the following way: "On 14 July violence broke out when a Kurdish mob supported by the People's Resistance Forces attacked a Turkish coffee shop because they objected to some Turkish writing on a decorative arch. The coffee shop was destroyed and the owner killed. This led to a general attack on the Turkish quarter in which a number of leading Turks were killed and shops and public buildings were set on fire. The mob had obtained arms from a police station which they had attacked. Kurdish troops of the Second Division joined with the mob and the People's Resistance Forces in attacks on the Turks. A curfew was imposed by the government but this was ignored by the Kurds. Some of the Turkish community managed to barricade themselves inside the citadel. On 15 July Kirkuk remained in the hands of the Kurdish mob and the People's Resistance Forces throughout the day. The mob tried to attack the Turks in the citadel and they were supported by dissident troops of the Second Division. On 16 July government reinforcements arrived under the command of Colonel Abdul Rahman Arif, Director of the Armoured Corps. He ordered troops of the Second Division to barracks and the People's Resistance Forces to their homes. Preliminary steps to restore order were taken and the Turks were persuaded to leave the citadel. The Commander of the Nineteenth Infantry Brigade, Abdul Karim Mohammed, arrived from Baghdad and took over command of the Second Division."[135]

As more detailed reports of the atrocities became known, Kassem openly condemned the action and expressed his determination to punish the guilty. The Kirkuk massacre demonstrated that ethnic animosity was strong enough to bring disaster, and it endangered the national unity in the country. The Iraqi premier, referring to the Kirkuk massacre in a press conference he held on July 29, 1959, stated, "Hulagu in his time did not commit such atrocities. We will show you some pictures of these atrocities." Kassem then produced a number of pictures taken during the massacre and showed them to the journalists, declaring, "These are the sons of our people. Are these the actions of the nationalist forces or the organisations which allege themselves to be democratic? These pictures indicate barbarity. Where are the plots? Is this reaction? Are your Turcoman brethren the enemies of the people? Pictures taken during the incidents convict certain groups. Take a look at these savage actions which have emanated from the sons of one people." And he added, "The police found maps with the names of the Kirkuk victims marked on them. Using the maps, murderers went to these houses, called out their residents, and killed them." Kassem told the journalists off the record that casualties so far amounted to 121 killed and 140 seriously injured—all Turks.[136]

Trevelyan's and Hayman's accounts on incidents at Kirkuk between July 14 and 16, 1959, are confirmed by the despatches of the then American ambassador in Baghdad, John Jernegan, and of other United States representatives in London and Ankara. On July 17, 1959, Jernegan informed the Department of State that reports reaching them belatedly and indirectly indicated that very serious disorder broke out in Kirkuk on July 14 and that the city was now under tight security control. A twenty-four-hour curfew had been in effect since July 16. Army reinforcements had been sent to Kirkuk, which was the headquarters of the Second Division and regularly garrisoned by the Fourth Brigade. About twenty doctors were sent from Baghdad to help care for the casualties. It was first heard that junior officers, loyal to Brigadier Davoud al-Janabi, commander of the Second Division, whose "retirement," for procommunist bias, was announced on June 30, had begun an intra-army fight. This story was doubted since nine officers from al-Janabi's headquarters, ranging from lieutenant colonels to lieutenants, were "retired" on the first days of July in an obvious effort by Kassem to clean out unreliable elements at the division headquarters. More plausible were later reports that trouble centred on large-scale clashes between Turcoman and Kurdish communities in Kirkuk. Communal tension had been simmering since the riots of October 25, 1958.[137]

During a speech at the Chaldean church in Baghdad on July 19, 1959, Premier Kassem took a strong line and had the following to say: "The recent events in Kirkuk are things which I utterly condemn. We are capable, brothers, of crushing anyone who comes up against our people with acts of anarchy stemming from feuds, grudges and blind fanaticism. I will bring to serve account those who trespassed on the freedom of the people of Kirkuk."[138]

On July 22, 1959, a representative of the United States embassy in London discussed the current situation in Kirkuk with C. M. Le Quesne, assistant head of the Eastern Department of the British Foreign Office. Le Quesne said that there was no evidence of disorder premeditated or instigated from outside Kirkuk itself. He laid stress on the existing antagonisms in the city between the Turcoman and Kurdish communities and the general excitement generated by the July 14 celebrations. Communists had endeavoured to capitalise on the opportunity presented. The army unit, which had been deployed, was mainly composed of Kurds, who should have been expected to be less than effective against other Kurds.[139]

Neither the radio nor the press in Baghdad published certain off-the-record statements that Kassem made at a landmark press conference on July

29, 1959. Most striking of these, as passed to the United States embassy by the American newsmen who got them from the Iraqis who were present, was, "These pictures alone would have been enough to bring about foreign intervention. But the foreign powers know that I am taking action." Kassem said this as he passed around the table photographs of eighty-one bodies of Turcomans killed in Kirkuk incidents. Kassem said that what happened at Kirkuk had made him physically ill. He was out of circulation for two or three days the previous week. Elaborating on his off-the-record remark about the possibility that the Kirkuk slaughter could have triggered a foreign intervention, Kassem said on-record that if it had not been for Radio Baghdad's repeated broadcasts of his speeches, Iraq's reputation in the outside world would have been nil.[140]

Kassem summoned representatives of the Iraqi trade unions and "popular organisations" to his office on August 29, 1959, and lectured them for three hours. On the Kirkuk massacre he said the following: "Kirkuk incidents are a black smear on our history. Is this the civilisation of the twentieth century? Would anyone of you agree to be a member of the government which approved such atrocities? Seventy-nine persons were killed in these incidents in addition to forty-one injured, some of whom were buried alive. We could save only three."[141]

According to a telegram sent by Fletcher Warren, the American ambassador in Ankara, to the Department of State on August 29, 1959, during a normal exchange with an embassy representative on July 29, Refik İleri, second department officer of the Turkish Ministry of Foreign Affairs said that further reports regarding the Kirkuk violence now clearly indicated that the origin of the disturbance lay in Turcoman-Kurdish intercommunal antagonism. İleri stated that communists doubtless sought to exploit the incidents but insisted, as his personal view, that the source of the trouble was not primarily political but ethnic. Kurds' long-standing aim, he continued, was simply the elimination of all non-Kurdish elements from northern Iraq, which they regard as part of "Kurdistan" homeland. Kurdish hatred and jealousy against the Turcoman community is exacerbated by differences in economic and cultural status.[142]

The worst happened. It was the most grisly ethnic clash since the proclamation of the republic. A large number of murders added fuel to the ethnic fire. The underlying structural stresses produced outer tremors. The Kirkuk massacre has both expressed and exacerbated the tensions between the Turcomans and the Kurds. In the opinion of Phebe Marr, author of a seminal work on Iraq, traditional animosities festering beneath the surface between the Turcomans and the Kurds erupted. The Kurdish communists, soldiers, and tribesmen were responsible for most of the deaths.[143] Marr's point is a valid one. Majid Khadduri, an Iraqi Christian jurist and historian, has indicated that most dramatically, according to one report, forty persons were buried alive by the Kurdish communists.[144] The so-called purge of Kirkuk of July 14-16, 1959, had profound political and psychological consequences. It left deep scars that proved to be very slow to heal over the past forty-seven years. The memory became irradicably etched on the minds of the Turcomans. The enmities arising out of this conflict were hard for the Turcomans to forget and are still the major source of Turcoman mistrust towards the Kurds.

CHAPTER V

GROSS HUMAN RIGHTS VIOLATIONS
AGAINST THE TURCOMANS

FEW PEOPLES IN modern times have suffered as grievously as the Iraqi Turcomans. From the first day of the creation of the Iraqi state, the Turcomans had been marginalised and subjected to all levels of repression and assimilation, which they resisted in every possible way. Although the Treaty of Alliance of October 10, 1922, between Iraq and Britain guaranteed, in Article 3, that there would be no racial, linguistic, or religious discrimination and that each community should have schools teaching in its own language, the problem of the rights of the Turcomans was a matter of little concern.[145] The outbreak of arrogant and tactless Assyrian levies in Kirkuk on May 4, 1924, when many innocent Turcomans were murdered, has not been forgotten, and the memory still rankles.

A dispute over the price of a few kilograms of sugar between men of the Second Assyrian Levy Battalion, a unit which was composed of the wildest elements, and a Turcoman shopkeeper in the bazaar flared up to a fight. The sudden disturbance spread like a grassfire, and soon it became a full-scale massacre of Turcomans. These troops were all hill men. They assaulted a number of Turcomans who were sitting in a coffee shop. Tension ran high, and the news was carried back to the barracks that an Assyrian soldier had been killed, and this news set the match to the powder barrel.[146]

The Assyrian soldiers rushed back to their quarters, spread the alarm, and, seizing their rifles and ammunition, put into practice the emergency drill—which amounted to seizing the strategic points in the town, chief of which was a house situated on the highest point in the citadel on which the old part of the town was built. From this point, they commanded the bridge across the river and the roads going north and south and proceeded to shoot as many of the Turcomans as came into view. They ran amok through the town for some three hours, firing at and killing all Turcomans they met. On such occasions the casualties are difficult to assess, and the most reliable estimate was reckoned at 280 dead.[147]

The Turcomans faced massacres and ethnic cleansing, which had the highest number of casualties during Saddam Hussein's reign of terror. Rights the Iraqi government had itself agreed to respect—those guaranteed in the International Covenant on Civil and Political Rights, for example and the nation's own constitution—had been consistently ignored by various organs of the Baath Party.[148] Rights to life, expression, movement, and association have been violated on a regular basis through killings, disappearances, and deportations. The Turcomans have been expelled from Kirkuk and the surrounding areas for at least thirty-five years and replaced in many cases by landless Arab settlers from the nearby Jazira desert and other parts of Iraq, who were forced to move by the Baath Party or lured to formerly Turcoman neighbourhoods with subsidised housing. The majority of deportees were removed to desert locations in southern Iraq; many were abandoned without any shelter. Others were housed in rudimentary camps along major routes under military control. The process of forced expulsions from Kirkuk was a centrally organised, bureaucratic government campaign, involving formal documents such as the expulsion orders many victims received. Baathi leadership therefore committed offences against international humanitarian law. Any amount of primary evidence to that effect is available.

Human rights are entitlements due to every man, woman, and child because they are human. They include rights pertaining to the security of the person, including the right not to be deprived of life or liberty without due process of law; the right not to be tortured or subjected to cruel, inhuman, or degrading treatment or punishment; and the right not to be held in slavery or servitude. They are nonderogable rights: Their violation can never be justified, even by a state of national emergency. Human rights also include civil and political rights, among them the right to freedom of thought, conscience, and religion; the right to freedom of opinion and expression; the right to freedom of peaceful assembly and association; the right to freedom of movement; and the right to take part in the government of one's own country, directly or through freely chosen representatives. There are also economic, social, and cultural rights to which everyone is entitled. These include basic survival rights to food, shelter, health care, and social services; the right to work; the right to education; and the right to participate in the cultural life of one's community. The premise of current international law is that these rights are inherent in the human person.

Human rights have a prominent place on the international agenda; the UN has been entrusted with enormous responsibilities for managing human rights. Since it first met in 1947, the UN Commission on Human Rights has been at the forefront of international activity to define, promote, and protect human rights and fundamental freedoms. In addition to preparing a number of international treaties and declarations, the commission has considered many situations involving violations of those rights and freedoms; has sought, through persuasion and dialogue, to prevent and eliminate human rights violations; has recommended measures to ensure compliance with universally recognised norms of human rights; and has offered and provided, upon request, advisory services and other expert assistance to reduce the incidence of violation of human rights.

In addition to debating and taking action on items on the agenda of its annual sessions, the UN Commission on Human Rights has developed a variety of mechanisms that enable it to carry out its work effectively. On many occasions, it has called upon one or more of its members, or other qualified experts, to perform fact-finding tasks, designating them as special rapporteurs, special representatives, or special envoys. These experts, acting in their personal capacity, have examined questions relating to thematic human rights issues, such as summary and arbitrary executions, torture and intolerance based on religion or ethnicity. They have also examined the human rights situation in particular countries.

The best accessible source on Iraq's abuse of human rights seems to be the reports of competent but substantially disinterested UN special rapporteur on human rights. The value of this documentation is worth emphasising. It deserves the careful attention of all those interested in Iraqi affairs. The relevance of these basic observations is important to the understanding of the situation of the human rights of the Turcomans. They constitute an invaluable wealth of information on the Turcoman condition at the time. These documents provide an effective response to those who would obscure or deny the truth of the Turcoman plight.

At its forty-seventh session, the Commission on Human Rights adopted resolution 1991/74 of March 6, 1991, entitled "Situation on human rights in Iraq." As a result of that resolution, and upon its approval by decision 1991/256 of March 31, 1991, of the Economic and Social Council, the chairman of the commission appointed Max van der Stoel on June 25, 1991, to serve as special rapporteur of the Commission on Human Rights on the situation of human rights in Iraq. Thereupon, van der Stoel took up his duties as defined in resolution 1991/74 and submitted on November 13, 1991, an interim report (A/46/647) to the forty-sixth session of the General Assembly and, on February 18, 1991, a full report (E/CN.4/1992/31) to the forty-eighth session of the Commission on Human Rights.[149]

The special rapporteur van der Stoel, in his report of November 18, 1991, was concerned about the protection of the Turcoman community. The free use of the Turcomans' language remained in doubt in view of the failure of the Iraqi government so far to respond to the specific questions on this matter. The special rapporteur was similarly concerned about the restrictions on the participation of the Turcomans in the public institutions and governments of those regions where they constituted a large part of the population. Furthermore, the special rapporteur was worried about those practices that obliged a Turcoman to sell his real estate only to an Arab as part of a policy aimed at altering the ethnic ratios of the regions.[150]

The special rapporteur van der Stoel, in his report of February 18, 1992, noted that the Turcomans were the third largest ethnic group in Iraq. Originally from central Asia, they began settling in Iraq one thousand years ago and still inhabited the north and middle of Iraq, concentrated mainly in the provinces of Mosul, Arbil, Kirkuk, and Diyala. The special rapporteur pointed out that at present they numbered some two million people. An Iraqi government declaration on the rights of ethnic minorities, dated January 24, 1970, originally permitted the use of the Turkish language in primary education and in newspapers and magazines. The Turcoman community was also granted permission for the broadcasting of radio and television programmes. However, all of these rights were withdrawn a year later, and the Turcoman population was subjected to systematic discrimination and abuse.[151]

According to the same report, oppression and persecution against the Turcomans included arrest without charge, torture, internal deportation and exile, confiscation of personal and community properties, and execution. Such oppression and persecution originated in a government policy to replace the Turcomans with Arabs in Kirkuk and other cities and towns where the Turcomans were especially represented. In particular, Turcoman citizens of Kirkuk were subjected to restrictions on the purchase and sale of real estate: They were allowed to sell only to Arabs. The Turcomans were also forced to leave their lands in the regions they had been inhabiting for centuries. Contrary to official statements claiming that the Turcomans were considered a minority and thus granted the right to exercise all their cultural rights, the Iraqi government obliged them to be registered either as Arabs or as Kurds. As such, the people were denied their rights as a Turcoman community.[152]

By the Commission on Human Rights resolution 1992/71 of March 5, 1992, as approved by the Economic and Social Council decision 1992/241 of July 20, 1992, the mandate of the special rapporteur was extended for a second year. In so extending the mandate of the special rapporteur, the exact terms of the mandate remained unchanged, which is to say that the special rapporteur was only to consider "violations by the government of Iraq" irrespective of any other violations relating to Iraq of which he might be, and was, aware. As in the first year, the special rapporteur was requested to submit an interim report to the General Assembly at its forty-seventh session and a full report to the Commission on Human Rights at its forty-ninth session. Beyond these requests, the special rapporteur was also specifically requested, "in consultation with the secretary-general, to develop further his recommendation for an exceptional response" and "in pursuing his mandate to visit again the northern area of Iraq, in particular."[153]

In accordance with his duties as an independent expert in the service of the Commission on Human Rights, the special rapporteur continued to study the situation of human rights in Iraq by drawing on all available means. Information was again received from a wide variety of sources. Besides both general and specific reports, the special rapporteur received testimonies from victims and eyewitnesses of alleged violations. Reports and testimonies were sometimes supported by documentary evidence in the form of photographs, video-cassettes, and official documents attributed to the government of Iraq. In examining this information, corroborative evidence was sought and obtained on many occasions. Alarmed by the seriousness of the many reports he had previously received, and having sought and obtained independent confirmation of several of the relevant facts, the special rapporteur appealed to the government of Iraq to cease those of its activities that were in violation of its obligations under international law.[154]

In studying and assessing the situation of human rights in Iraq, the special rapporteur has again applied only those standards of international human rights law that are applicable to Iraq as a result of undertakings of its own choosing, which is to say those standards articulated in the texts of the international human rights conventions to which Iraq has become a party. Aside from the explicit standards of such conventions, the special rapporteur has also applied such obligations as arose as a matter of international customary law. The obligations undertaken by Iraq as a result of its accession to human rights conventions include the following: the Charter of the UN; the International Covenant on Civil and Political Rights; the International Convention on the Elimination of All Forms of Racial Discrimination; the Convention on the Elimination of All Forms of Discrimination against Women; and the Convention on the Prevention and Punishment of the Crime of Genocide. Other important conventions to which Iraq has freely become a state party include the four Geneva Conventions of August 12, 1949, and the Constitution of the International Labour Organisation, together with various conventions developed under the auspices of that organisation such as Convention No. 98 of 1949 concerning the Application of the Principles of the Right to Organise and Bargain Collectively and Convention No. 107 of 1957 concerning the Protection and Integration of Indigenous and other Tribal and Semi-Tribunal Populations in Independent Countries.[155]

With respect to human rights obligations arising under the Charter of the UN, explicit obligations are found in the Preamble, Article 1, paragraph 3, Article 55 (c) and Article 56. Of these, the texts of the Preamble, articles 1 (3) and 55 (c) emphasise the obligation of nondiscrimination. Moreover, the texts of the Preamble and Article 1 (3) relate to the very object and purpose of the UN and therefore constitute primordial obligations of which no other action should supersede or detract. In this connection, and in terms of the specificity of the obligations arising from the Charter of the UN, the special rapporteur also noted the texts of various human rights declarations including the 1948 Universal Declaration of Human Rights, the 1959 Declaration on the Rights of the Child, the 1963 Declaration on the Elimination of All Forms of Racial Discrimination, the 1967 Declaration on the Elimination of Discrimination against Women, the 1974 Declaration on the Protection of Women and Children in Time of Emergency and Armed Conflict, the 1975 Declaration on the Protection of All Persons from Being Subjected to Torture and Other Cruel, Inhuman or Degrading Treatment or Punishment, the 1981 Declaration on the Elimination of All Forms of Intolerance and Discrimination Based on Religion or Belief, and the 1992 Declaration on the Rights of Persons Belonging to National or Ethnic, Religious and Linguistic Minorities.[156]

Having recounted the undertakings that the government of Iraq was obliged to uphold and respect as a matter of general international law according to the principle of *pacta sunt servanda*—which pertains as a fundamental tenet of international customary law and forms the basis of the Vienna Convention on the Law of Treaties of 1969—the special rapporteur could not ignore the peculiar situation that applied to Iraq as a matter of other obligations arising under international law. These obligations arose as a result of sanctions legally applied to Iraq subsequent to its grave breaches of the most fundamental obligations of general international law. In particular, the special rapporteur referred to Security Council resolutions 661 (1990), 666 (1990), 687 (1991), and 688 (1991). In addition, the special rapporteur took note of the related Security Council resolutions 706 and 712 of 1991 and 778 of 1992.[157]

The special rapporteur had to emphasise that the nature of the obligations freely undertaken by Iraq and articulated in the conventions referred to above were such as to have effectively reduced Iraq's sphere of sovereignty over these matters while at the same time enlarging the competence of the international community over these same matters. In specific terms, the obligations arising from the Charter include among the very objects and purposes of this most basic instrument "respect for human rights," which, therefore, necessarily meant (according to Article 31 of the Vienna Convention on the Law of Treaties) that the obligations of human rights could not be escaped on the basis of Article 2, paragraph 7 of the Charter, which relates to "matters which are essentially within the domestic jurisdiction of any state." In a similar fashion, obligations arising under other human rights conventions might not be avoided save for those specific obligations that were subject to permissible derogations and from which the government had derogated according to the relevant procedural and substantive requirements.[158]

In his report dated February 19, 1993, the special rapporteur expressed that the lot of the Turcoman population, who had never constituted real opposition in recent times, has been more that of a traditional ethnic and linguistic minority in search of commonly sought-after minority rights, such as the freedom to enjoy education and training in the Turkish language and to enjoy cultural and media programming in the same language. Indeed, aside from the various violations essentially in connection with language, culture, and property—and upon which the special rapporteur had previously reported—it was to be noted that the Turcoman population also sought recognition of its identity before the law in so far as this had not been accorded and in so far as Article 6 of the Provisional Constitution of Iraq declared that "the people of Iraq consists of Arabs and Kurds."[159]

The most fundamental issue concerned recognition of the group, that is to say, the right of members of the Turcoman community to be recognised before the law as Turcomans, together with the group per se. Thus in the special rapporteur's most comprehensive report on the subject presented to the UN Commission on Human Rights, it is particularly emphasised that "although the Turcoman population constitutes the third largest ethnic community in Iraq with an historical presence dating back one thousand years chiefly in the north central plains of the country, the group still faces the rudimentary problem of official recognition of its identity, for instance, of nonaccommodation in the national censuses and denial of linguistic rights even in places where the Turcomans form an overwhelming majority."[160]

According to the 1970 Provisional Constitution, Iraq was composed principally of Arabs and Kurds with minorities entitled to only those rights that would not conflict with Iraqi unity. Revolutionary Command Council decree No. 89 of January 24, 1970, granted some cultural rights to Iraqi Turcomans. However, neither of the 1977 and 1987 national censuses provided for any identity other than "Arab" or "Kurd," requiring specification of one or the other. Turcomans were compelled by census agents to identify themselves as Arabs. While this decree provided the Turcoman community with a number of cultural rights, it was barely implemented at the time of its promulgation and was followed, after 1972, with a programme of discrimination, repression, and strict government control. Since that date educational and cultural institutions of the Turcoman community have either been closed or subjected to direct or indirect government controls. For example, the government had closed down Turcoman schools and forbidden studies in the Turkish language. There was no Turkish media in Iraq, save for one government-controlled radio station in Baghdad. Since 1975, Turcoman cultural societies had their directors replaced by pro-government Baath Party members. Turcoman clergymen were forbidden to speak or lead prayers in the Turkish language. With regard to physical properties, new Turcoman mosques were required to carry Arabic designs and script; some mosques and ancient properties were destroyed in whole or in part under various pretexts.[161]

Administrative boundaries were changed in 1974 to divide Turcoman concentrations. Since the mid-1970s, Arabs have enjoyed special incentives and rights encouraging them to move to historically Turcoman areas, especially the cities of Kirkuk and Mosul. In the second half of the 1970s, several villages and places in the governorate of Kirkuk were given Arabic names; and in the 1980s, Turcoman societies, institutions, and properties were officially Arabised. Arabs were granted privileges as enticements to move to Kirkuk and Mosul, while non-Arabs were restricted in the options for conveyance of real estate, change of residence, etc. Discriminatory measures in the transfer of property rights were applied in relation to the Turcoman community.[162]

In the UN report of February 25, 1994, it is also mentioned that many violations have been suffered by ethnic communities simply because they happened to be living in areas designated for a military campaign meant to exterminate political opposition in the region. For example, many Turcomans suffered destruction of their villages and monuments, arbitrary arrest and detention, torture, execution, and disappearance during the notorious Anfal campaign in 1988. In many cases, they were accused of collaboration with the Kurdish opposition thought to be in the area. Following the uprising in northern Iraq in March 1991, members of the Turcoman community have come under renewed suspicion.[163]

Again according to this report, several Turcomans were executed near Kirkuk at the end of June 1993. Their bodies, which were returned to the families almost three weeks after execution, bore marks of severe torture. A very large number of Turcoman families in Kirkuk were given deportation notifications at the end of November 1993. Families perceived to be opposed to the regime, families who had relatives outside Iraq or in southern Iraq, and those who had relatives who were either in detention or executed were the first targeted in the process of forced displacement. Fifteen families were deported to the northern area without any belongings, while twenty-five families were driven to southern governorates with small amounts of their belongings. Their property was confiscated by the government and often taken for the personal use of government officials. In many cases, local administrators and those directly involved in the confiscations were given their share. In the town of Tuzhurmatu, where the call for prayer was prohibited after the March 1991 uprisings, at least two mosques, including the main one, were closed by the government. In one Turcoman quarter of Kirkuk called District of Ninety, four mosques were demolished, and most of the estimated twenty-five-thousand population have been relocated to other places. It was the first time that the Turcomans had ever been so prominently mentioned in a UN document.[164]

Another report by the UN, dated November 8, 1996, further spells out problems confronting the Turcomans. They had been subjected to constant oppression and persecution. These acts included arrest without charge, internal deportation or exile, and confiscation of personal property and a government policy to forcibly replace the Turcomans with Arabs in Kirkuk and the surrounding area, part of a process known as Arabisation. In addition, the Turcomans of Kirkuk had been subjected to restrictions on the purchase and sale of real estate; they had only been allowed to sell to Arabs.[165]

The UN report of October 15, 1997, notes that forcible relocations took place in the context of a policy aimed at systematically changing the demography of Kirkuk by deporting Turcoman families en masse. In order to increase the percentage of the Arab population in the predominantly Turcoman areas, the Iraqi government forced entire communities to undergo internal deportation. Those expelled included individuals who had refused to sign the so-called nationality correction forms—introduced by the authorities prior to the 1997 population census—requiring members of ethnic groups residing in these districts to relinquish their Turcoman or Kurdish identities and to register officially as Arabs. The Iraqi authorities also seized their properties and assets. Heads of households were often detained until the expulsions were complete. The real estate and personal property left by the deportees was then given to Arabs coming from other parts of Iraq. Several Turcoman villages were entirely destroyed. Cases of forced eviction and deportation occurred with great frequency and as a matter of policy. They were given, at most, one week's notice to move and were threatened with arrest if they did not comply.[166]

Also according to this report, the expropriation of Turcoman agricultural land had become commonplace. People whose lands were expropriated were paid a sum not even equivalent to one year's yield. Ownership of the land had allegedly been transferred to high-level officials of the regime, including some of Saddam Hussein's family. Although the practice of forced relocation and deportation by the government of Iraq to decrease the presence of the Turcoman and Kurdish population living in that area and to strengthen their hold on the important economic and strategic governorate of Kirkuk was not new, the scale of these activities increased in 1997. Forced expulsion had long been a tool of the Iraqi government. Since the late 1960s, Saddam Hussein's Baath Party relocated huge segments of Iraq's population from place to place, either to suppress uprisings or to skew demographics near oil fields in favour of the ruling Arab class.[167]

The report filed by special rapporteur van der Stoel in 1998 did not differ from the preceding one. Turcoman families were required to move to the central and southern parts of the country. They were relocated to barren sites, where they had to rebuild their lives from scratch. At the same time, Arabs were encouraged to settle in Kirkuk; their proportion has increased. Arabs were given incentives of money and apartments to settle in Kirkuk. Baath Party members were responsible for the implementation of the decisions. Moreover, authorities openly discriminated against non-Arabs in the educational system, civil administration, and even in the granting of Iraqi citizenship. Regions were renamed, stressing their Arab rather than non-Arab connections; various areas were designated as military and security zones from which groups could be more easily expelled, and particular districts were mined in order to restrict and prevent the return of those removed from their traditional places of residence.[168] In the United States State Department's 2003 year report on human rights practices in Iraq, it is estimated that hundreds of thousands of citizens were forcibly displaced under Saddam Hussein and large numbers of these compulsory relocations occurred in Kirkuk.[169]

Since the submission of his previous report to the Commission on Human Rights, the special rapporteur continued to receive allegations describing the deteriorating human rights situation of the Turcomans of the governorate of Kirkuk. In particular, the government of Iraq continued to implement its policy of Arabisation in Kirkuk. However, simultaneous campaigns were also under way in the districts of Khanaqin, Makhmour, Sinjar, and Sheikhan. Non-Arab citizens were denied equal access to employment and educational opportunities and were also physically threatened. For example, employment in the public administration, including the national oil company (the largest employer in the region), was effectively reserved for citizens of Arab origin. Deterrent measures, such as the relocation of Turcoman elementary school teachers and low-ranking civil servants to areas outside Kirkuk, were also part of the regime's policy of modifying the demography of the region. Other discriminatory measures were applied by the local administration of Kirkuk: New construction or renovation of existing Turcoman property was forbidden, and the Turcomans were prevented from registering or inheriting properties. At the same time, Arab settlement was favoured. The Revolutionary Command Council mandated that the government must provide new housing and employment to more than three hundred thousand Arab residents settled in Kirkuk. In 1998 at least seven new Arab settlements were built on properties confiscated from non-Arabs. The new settlements were given Arab names, and local merchants were instructed to give their companies Arab names. Finally, the governorate's administrative offices were moved to the Arabised side of the city, as were the headquarters of major professional and political organisations.[170]

The government of Iraq used other measures aimed at encouraging departures and preventing displaced persons from returning. The government declared the area around Kirkuk, including the oil fields and production facilities, a military and security zone and mined the area to impede transit. The roads into the area were heavily fortified with military checkpoints. In 1998, the Iraqi government evicted the residents of Kirkuk's citadel and began the demolition of this ancient Turcoman site, claiming that the envisioned new construction would generate considerable tourist revenue.[171]

Meanwhile, the European Parliament in its resolution "Situation in Iraq eleven years after the Gulf war," dated May 16, 2002, stated that the Iraqi government had committed gross and massive human rights violations, including an active policy of persecution of the Kurdish, Turcoman, and

Assyrian populations in the north. It was also noted that a policy of Arabisation and ethnic cleansing was followed in the regions of Kirkuk, Sinjar, Mandali, Jalawla, and Mosul; and over eight hundred thousand persons of Kurdish, Turcoman, and Assyro-Chaldean identity were internally displaced.[172]

More than three and a half years have passed since the coalition forces liberated Iraq from the worst dictator ever known in Iraqi history. Like the rest of the Iraqi people, the Turcomans were jubilant when this historic event took place. They were happy to see the end of the tyrant who had made their lives so miserable for such a long time and the lifting of thirteen years of economic sanctions that had inflicted severe hardship on the country's population. A government that preyed on the Iraqi people and committed shocking systematic and criminal violations of human rights was removed. The Turcomans expected democracy to be established and free elections held so that a national government would be created from the people, by the people, and for the people—a government that disregarded ethnic and sectarian divisions, whose only aim would have been to heal the wounded Iraqi nation. They hoped that the new government would not make differences between them and other nationalities, but consider all of them as one—the same laws and same rights for all Iraqis. That did not really happen. The actual achievement of democracy in Iraq remains distant and uncertain.

Events worsened. Both Kirkuk and its hinterlands remain rife with disorder and uncertainty. Turmoil is increasingly invading the city. There is scant evidence that the overall dire security situation is going to improve. These developments are watched with increasing anxiety. Turcoman leaders called on March 1, 2004, for international help in keeping the peace in Kirkuk where ethnic tensions between the Turcomans and the Kurds had flared. They demanded that the UN, the Arab League, and the Organisation of the Islamic Conference should send peace-keeping forces to maintain security in Kirkuk to prevent events which could lead to civil war.[173]

The UN secretary-general received on February 11, 2005, the written statement entitled "Racism, racial discrimination, xenophobia and all forms of discrimination: comprehensive implementation of and follow-up to the Durban Declaration and Programme of Action" from the Transnational Radical Party—a nongovernmental organisation in general consultative status—which was circulated in accordance with Economic and Social Council resolution 1996/31. The aforesaid party wished to address the human rights situation in Iraq, in particular concerning the Iraqi Turcomans. The very existence of the Turcomans in Iraq was at a critical juncture today with the rapid developments following the fall of Saddam Hussein's regime on April 9, 2003.

The Turcomans, in their long history in Iraq, have been downgraded from being masters and rulers of entire regions to an unrepresented and forgotten minority that is under constant assimilation pressure in these days.[174]

The statement noted that the Iraqi Turcomans, often confused with the Turcomans of central Asia, live in an area that they call *Turkmenia* in Latin or *Türkmeneli* which means "land of the Türkmens." It was referred to as Turcomania by the British geographer William Guthrie in 1785. The Turcomans are a Turkic group that has a unique heritage and culture as well as linguistic, historical, and cultural links with the surrounding Turkic groups such as those in Turkey and Azerbaijan. Their spoken and written language is like the Turkish used in present-day Anatolia. Their true population proportion has always been concealed by the authorities in Iraq for political reasons and estimated at only 2 percent, whereas in reality their number should be put between 2.5 to 3 million, that is to say 12 percent of the Iraqi population. The areas where the Turcomans live are oil-rich, which have made them the target of assimilation campaigns by neighbouring Arabs and Kurds.[175]

In the statement, it is mentioned that over the centuries, the Turcomans played a constructive role in Iraq, either by defending the country against foreign invaders or bringing civilisation. Their monuments and architectural remains exist all over Iraq. They lived in harmony with all ethnic groups around them. They administered the people with justice and tolerance. There is no record in history of any mistreatment by the Turcomans of any of their subjects. On the contrary, they became relatives with other ethnicities through intermarriage. However, after the British invasion of Iraq in 1918, the Turcomans began to experience a different situation. Branded unjustly as loyal to Turkey, they were removed from the administration, pushed into isolation, and ignored. Then their fundamental human rights in culture and education were violated by the closure of their schools from 1933 to 1937. In 1959 they were racially discriminated against, and their fundamental political human rights were violated by excluding them from constitutional rights given to the Kurds. On July 14, 1959, they faced mass executions by the communists and the Kurds. In the 1970s and 1980s, they were subjected to ethnic cleansing by the Baath Party.[176]

The statement indicated that Arab racism reached such heights as to ban spoken Turcoman in public; Turcoman names of persons and locations were changed, while the historical monuments of Turcomans and their towns and villages faced destruction. Many Turcomans were relocated to southern Iraq. Thousands of Turcoman houses, lands, and properties were confiscated. They were even forced to change their nationality and were banned from purchasing property or repairing their homes. With the American invasion of Iraq, the statement continued, the Turcomans had high expectations from the interim administration established after April 9, 2003. They expected to see democracy, fairness, and an end to the discrimination and violence. Unfortunately, the opposite has happened. The Turcomans, led by their political parties; the Iraqi Turcoman Front; and the Turcoman Nationalist Movement, have expressed their opposition and have demonstrated peacefully against the new discrimination policies on several occasions in Kirkuk, Tuzhurmatu, and Baghdad, only to be shot at by Kurdish militias and American troops, turning those peaceful demonstrations into a bloodbath. Moreover, to break the Turcoman resistance completely, Talafar, which is overwhelmingly Turcoman, was attacked in September 2004 by Kurdish militias and bombarded heavily by American forces under the pretext of presence of foreign jihadists/terrorists, a threat that turned out to be wrong. The statement also emphasised that the Turcomans were forced to live under the mercy of other groups, who have not demonstrated a sincere desire to include the Turcomans in the development of a democratic Iraq.[177]

According to the same statement, in the elections of January 30, 2005—carried out in the absence of sufficient international observers—there were fears that several irregularities may have taken place in northern Iraq. For instance, despite the closure of registrations after January 23, 2005, one hundred thousand Kurds, who were not residents of Kirkuk, were registered three days later with the encouragement of foreign diplomats. Apparently, four hundred thousand people were denied their voting rights in the Turcoman region of Talafar and the Christian region of Bakhdeda; more than one hundred thousand Kurds were transported into Kirkuk, despite a ban on transportations from Arbil and Sulaimaniya on the occasion of the elections. Representatives of the Turcomans have protested to the "Independent Election Committee," but to no avail. There is the risk that the Turcomans may face assimilation pressures and Kurdification campaigns, which might deteriorate the relationship between the groups, triggering armed resistance. The statement concludes that it is therefore vital and of utmost importance that the UN, starting from the Commission on Human Rights, get involved in the situation in Iraq, including in future elections in the country.[178]

CONCLUSION

REGRETTABLY, IN TERMS of governmental actions towards the Turcomans, the history of modern Iraq has indeed often been witness to instances of treatment that can reasonably be described as severely discriminatory, selective, and repressive. The Turcomans were dealt with harshly. The richness of their territories has been a source of trouble for the Turcomans for decades, making their desire to live under decently humane conditions a difficult proposition. Facing pressure and exile has long been a part of their existence.

The British, after occupying Iraq in 1918, tried to force them to assimilate into Arab and Kurdish societies. There were massacres of Turcomans by Assyrians and Kurds in 1924 and 1959, and successive Iraqi regimes dispersed the Turcomans from the area. They replaced them with Arabs from the south and west. Even during the moderate days of the Iraqi monarchy, Turcoman rights, as stipulated by the League of Nations, were not observed. Legal protections have been more honoured in the breach than in the observance. Post-1918 Turcoman history has been a litany of pain and sorrow. The Turcomans have endured some of the worst persecutions in modern times.

Despite the oppression they have suffered, the Turcomans have never resorted to violence. Yet since the establishment of the modern Iraqi state, officials worked to suppress the Turcoman presence in the country. Schools providing education in Turkish were closed; Turkish-language newspapers were banned; Turcoman cultural assets were destroyed; and Turcoman intellectuals were jailed, sent into exile, and even killed. The political, cultural, and administrative rights of the Turcomans were usurped. Turcoman villages and areas were wiped off the map, and residents driven away to the south. They lost their jobs. Thousands of young Turcomans were sent to the front lines during the Iraq-Iran war of 1980-1988 to face certain death.

Nearby Turcoman towns were hived off and attached to Arab provinces to reduce the Turcoman presence in the Kirkuk governorate. Even the name of the Kirkuk governorate was changed to *Tamim*, Arabic for nationalisation. For decades Iraq has forbidden the Turcoman community to teach its language and history. The Turcomans could not buy property, repair their houses in their homeland, speak their language on the streets or on the telephone, and choose Turkish names for their children. The government prohibited their businesses from using non-Arab names and even ordered the script on tombstones to be replaced with Arabic. In spite of all this, the Turcomans do not regard themselves as fundamentally anything other than Iraqis. The Turcomans fought in the Iraq-Iran war, proving that they were no less Iraqi than their Arab counterparts. They just want to have their corporate identity recognised and their human rights respected and, in particular, to be free from discrimination. They require constitutional and security guarantees that they will not be tyrannised again. The Turcomans are searching for rights equal to those given to Kurds.

Because of its oil deposits and potential role in the formation of a breakaway Kurdish state, Kirkuk is the most likely flashpoint for inter-ethnic conflict. Though impoverished and neglected over recent decades, Kirkuk is a treasure. The province yields 40 percent of Iraq's oil, 70 percent of its oil products, and much of its agriculture. It is also the origin of the Iraqi pipeline that pumps oil to the Mediterranean coast.

Tensions between the Turcomans and the Kurds stretch back decades. The former doubly worry that a Kurdish takeover of Kirkuk could produce a repeat of the 1959 massacre. The Turcomans have been targets of looting by armed Kurdish bands who entered Kirkuk as the city fell on April 10, 2003. Kurds are perpetually accused of armed attacks against Turcoman political offices, television stations, and cultural centres. Kirkuk is the hub of the oil-rich northern region. Since the United States invasion, the city has become the stage of an ethnic power struggle. Kurds are trying to solidify their presence in Kirkuk and attempting to wrest control of the city, at the expense of the Turcomans and the Arabs. It is thought that this could herald a concerted drive to build an independent Kurdish state in northern Iraq.

Some observers say that Kirkuk could be a model for national unity or could trigger a civil war; it is often compared to Sarajevo. It is also described as a powder keg with a combustible mix of ethnic rivalries that could turn into a Kosovo. Now Kirkuk is a centre on the brink. The city is an explosion waiting to happen. A violent move could detonate the mix. Kurds dominate the United States-appointed city council. The administration offices are manned by Kurds who refuse to speak any other language but Kurdish. The Kurds regard Kirkuk and the vast oil reserves beneath it as theirs, and many want it to become the capital of a federal Kurdish state within Iraq, or even an independent Kurdistan. The city has long been coveted by Kurds. It is claimed by the Kurds as an indisputably Kurdish city. Impetuous actions could set off a time bomb. A Kirkuk takeover would give a quantum leap to Kurdish ambitions. The Turcomans and the Arabs are as fiercely opposed to any such scheme. Some two thousand Turcomans and Arabs demonstrated in late December 2003 against any effort to incorporate the city into an autonomous province. Five people were reported killed and dozens wounded.

Current levels of violence in Kirkuk are relatively low compared with those of western Iraq and Mosul, but there are recurrent kidnappings and separate incidents between the Kurds on one hand and the Turcomans and the Arabs on the other. The situation in Kirkuk might deteriorate seriously, to include bloodshed, if an acceptable solution to all of the existing ethnic problems in the city is not identified sooner rather than later. In order to prevent further loss of confidence, it will be important for the Kurds to refrain from unilateral actions. One of the tension-reducing precautions would be the more determined implementation of some procedures already agreed by the parties in Kirkuk. Namely, the Iraqi Property Claims Commission and its proper functioning could have been a factor for optimism towards stability and even harmony in the Kirkuk province, but its progress has been inadequate at best. By the end of 2004, the commission had received 10,044 claims from the area. The commission's statistics show that judges have decided only twenty-five cases. Only two judges, both Kurds, were working on cases in Kirkuk.

Kurds are accused of emulating Saddam Hussein with a process of "Kurdishisation," shipping in Kurdish families who have never lived in Kirkuk and forcing out non-Kurdish families who have lived there for generations. Turcoman and Arab residents say that the Patriotic Union of Kurdistan and the Kurdistan Democratic Party have encouraged displaced Kurds in the northern governorates, or even in Iran and Syria, to move to Kirkuk regardless of their original place of residence, endeavouring to increase Kurdish numbers ahead of a census, elections, and a referendum on the area's disposition. They say that the vast majority of Kurds entering Kirkuk is not originally from the city. The ethnic balance of Kirkuk has been visibly changed by the Kurdish influx. Few dispute that by January 2005 around 150,000 Kurds have either returned to the city from elsewhere or moved there for the first time.

Efforts to alter the demographic structure of Kirkuk could lead to serious problems. To keep Kirkuk, the Kurds will have to confront the whole of Iraq. Iraq's neighbours have repeatedly warned Iraqi Kurds against changing the area's demographics. Although they acknowledge that the future of Kirkuk is an internal issue for Iraq, Iraq's neighbours insist that the inclusion of the city into the Kurdish zone is a question in which they intend to play a part. The current rebuilding process will naturally be influenced by the regional context.

Kirkuk has also enormous historical and political significance for the Turcomans. It is the city for which they have suffered and sacrificed so much. Kirkuk is the cultural centre for the Turcomans. The Turcomans consider Kirkuk to be their own ancestral capital and compete with the Kurds for the right to control the city's civil authorities. This northern city and its three hundred oil wells is one of the pressure points where the new Iraq could blow apart. Whoever controls Kirkuk potentially controls oil fields representing 40 percent of Iraq's proven reserves. Such wealth could render an independent Kurdish state economically viable. Kurdish control of the Kirkuk oil fields could encourage Kurds to break away from Baghdad and trigger new turmoil in the region. A violent outburst will not only contribute to the further destabilisation of Iraq but will add another dangerous element to an already highly unsettled Middle Eastern area.

The future status of the Kirkuk district is one of the most sensitive questions that the government in Baghdad will have to tackle. Until the end of 2004, the two main Kurdish political parties, the Kurdish Democratic Party and the Patriotic Union of Kurdistan, were refusing to field candidates for regional elections, because they contended that registration favoured Arabs who had been moved there during the Baathi era. But on January 4, 2005, Iraq's minister of foreign affairs, Hoshyar Zebari, said the two parties agreed to participate in the poll.

It is stated that the Kurds, who won 59 percent of the votes in the January 30, 2005 elections to the regional assembly, engineered their victory by bringing in a flood of Kurdish voters from the north and by using coercion to keep non-Kurdish voters away from the polls. They are accused of rigging the elections by settling more Kurds in Kirkuk than were expelled under Saddam Hussein's rule. There is little dispute that the electoral outcome has given Kurdish ambitions new momentum. The situation has reached dangerous proportions. It is feared that there exists the possibility that these gross changes in the demography of Kirkuk could trigger an ethnic confrontation, which has not been so far.

Many of the worst electoral irregularities took place in Kurdish-dominated areas, where thousands of Turcomans were not able to vote due to logistical and security difficulties. In some cases election organisers did not bother to send enough ballots to Turcoman villages. The Turcomans and the Arabs muttered darkly about irregularities at the elections. The Kurds themselves acknowledged that there were irregularities in the three current Kurdish governorates (Dohuk, Arbil, and Sulaimaniya), where the Patriotic Union of Kurdistan and the Kurdistan Democratic Party competed in the provincial elections. In one particular instance, the votes cast in the Patriotic Union of Kurdistan-controlled town of Köysanjak were more than double the number of registered electors, though there were plenty of allegations about Kurdistan Democratic Party misconduct elsewhere too.

An unofficial referendum carried out in parallel with the elections purported to show that almost two million Kurds—nearly 99 percent of those polled—really want outright independence rather than to be part of Iraq. Their leaders know that any move in that direction could bring catastrophe. Iraqi Kurds must forgo their dream of independence and sole control of oil in Kirkuk. The low level of participation in the elections among certain groups, the lack of voting in a series of provinces and manipulation in certain areas, including Kirkuk, have created an imbalance in the results. Consequently, the Iraqi parliament does not reflect the true proportions of Iraqi society. No Iraqi constituency should be excluded from the current political process. In this regard, the alienation of the Turcomans is undesirable.

The primary responsibility of the assembly elected on January 30, 2005, was to promulgate a permanent constitution that was acceptable to all Iraqis. The process of drafting this document should have been inclusive and involved meritorious representatives of Iraq's communities. Even though the Turcomans were underrepresented in the assembly, the Iraqi government should have made sure they were sufficiently included in the constitutional committee. In addition to assembly members, well-respected Turcomans—including lawyers, technocrats, and specialists—with communications and community outreach skills should have participated in the committee. That did not really happen. However, with adequate Turcoman involvement, the steps planned for 2007, could become positive benchmarks in building a democratic and stable Iraq. But if most of Iraq's Turcomans remain distrustful and estranged, these steps could bring increased tension and divisiveness, raising the risk of eventual civil conflict.

Iraq's new constitution was signed on August 28, 2005, by a committee composed of Kurds and Shiite Arabs, bypassing Sunni Arabs' objections to provisions that allow for the establishment of regional autonomous zones with few ties to the central government. After two months of wrangling, intense pressure from the United States and a few last-minute amendments, the constitution's drafters ultimately failed to come up with a unified vision for ruling the new Iraq. The constitution creates a loose federal structure modelled after the currently semiautonomous Kurdish north. Provinces can join to form regional governments allowed to establish their own courts and local security forces, define the role of Islam in local law, and have some say in the distribution of oil wealth and trade. The central government's powers are limited largely to foreign policy and fiscal issues. As for the communal rights of the Turcomans, the whole thing the constitution mentions is that of the right "of educating their children in their mother tongue and of having the Turcoman language as one of the official languages in the administrative units in which they represent density of population."

The future status of Kirkuk has not been settled yet. The most contentious constitutional question has been deferred, at the latest till the end of 2007. It is left to next legitimately elected parliaments. As it should be. The parliamentary committee fashioning the constitution was not sufficiently representative to have the last say on this sensitive issue. The Kurdish demand for a referendum on the governance of the city also remains an open and heavily debated question.

Iraq is considered one of the biggest oil producers and exporters in the world. However, since 1980 its oil industry has suffered significantly from wars, sanctions, negligence and lack of maintenance, and—since the second Gulf war—from sabotage and looting. As a result the industry faces a number of challenges; but with the provision of security and finance, it has huge positive prospects. Security is the most important problem regarding the oil industry. During the last three years the oil facilities have suffered numerous attacks, leaving negative effects on the industry. Sabotage and looting continue to restrict progress on increasing oil exports and the availability of domestic fuel from Iraqi refineries. Despite its huge reserves, Iraq suffers from an endemic shortage of refined oil products, forcing it to import half its gasoline and thousands of tons of other refined products such as heating fuel and cooking gas. According to an Iraqi Ministry of Oil spokesman, the country has suffered damage to oil infrastructure and subsequently lost oil exports worth 11.5 billion dollars since the United States invasion in 2003. Speaking on July 3, 2005, the official said that Iraqi oil infrastructure had suffered three hundred attacks since June 2003, with seventy of those taking place in the first months of 2005.

The outcome of these attacks on the Iraqi economy can be summarised as follows: The loss of oil revenues and the damage to oil facilities has been in the order of four to five billion dollars annually. As oil prices continue to climb, the loss of potential revenue grows. Interruption of crude supplies has affected the flow of oil to refineries and power plants. Continuous attacks on the northern pipelines have affected the flow of oil exports to Turkey. Iraq's oil production and exports have become difficult to predict. Foreign and local investments in the oil industry are discouraged. Rehabilitating/expanding operations and facilities have become difficult. It has been estimated that almost 40 percent of the total costs of economic projects in Iraq goes to security. And lack of security encourages smuggling of both crude oil and oil products.

No one doubts northern Iraq's potential for enormous oil production. Only few known oil fields have been developed, and the costs of new production are among the world's lowest. Huge geologically promising areas of the region have never been explored with advanced seismic techniques. But the focus now is simply on resuming maintenance at existing fields to safeguard their output. Since the international sanctions that followed Iraq's invasion of Kuwait on August 2, 1990, the country has done virtually none of the customary nurturing of oil wells normally carried out every one to three years. Also halted was the drilling of new wells, which is necessary to replace old ones, to reach shifting reservoir pockets or to apply strategic injections of pressure. Some oil specialists note that even if Iraq's political situation stabilises, it will take years to sign contracts and dig new oil wells. Any major decision on oil development must also await the results of a study, being conducted by British Petroleum and Royal Dutch Shell, that will chart the state of the country's oil fields and assess the most promising next steps.

Turkey is an important route for the export of oil from northern Iraq. Attacks on the northern oil pipelines have halted the export of crude via Turkey and the shipment of crude from Kirkuk to Baghdad, limiting northern crude production to the amount that can be refined at the Baiji and Kirkuk refineries and shipped to Baghdad via truck. The impact of these problems meant that crude production and export in 2005 remained little changed from that of 2004. Continued attacks on the northern oil pipelines and the almost complete outage of the twenty-two-inch pipeline that is used to transport products from the Baiji refinery to the Baghdad area precipitated a near crisis in fuel availability during the month prior to the January 30, 2005 elections.

By the end of the decade, depending on the circumstances, Iraq could be shipping a large volume of crude through its dual pipeline running from Kirkuk. During an oil conference in April 2005 in the United States, Iraqi Minister of State Adnan al-Janabi said, "Strategically, Iraq should go the Mediterranean" with its future oil exports. The Iraqi crude export system through Turkey has a design capacity of 1.6 million barrels per day; but after so many years of inadequate maintenance and insurgent attacks, it would require recommissioning to reach that level. At Yumurtalık, Turkey has twelve storage tanks committed to Iraqi oil. Each has a capacity of 135,000 cubic metres, or 85,000 barrels, giving the terminal a current capacity to hold more than ten million barrels of Iraqi crude.

While the Kurds are continuing to assert their claim on the Kirkuk oil fields, no future government in Baghdad would countenance them slipping out of state control. Kirkuk is a thorny political issue. But as far as oil is concerned, it is a red line with regard to Iraqi officials. Without control of Kirkuk, the Kurds would have only a small oil card to play. At present, the only operating field in the Kurdish-controlled area is Taqtaq, with production averaging 2,000 barrels per day. In the early 1990s, the central government established a small tapping plant at Köysanjak, which is being expanded.

The Turcomans feel they have been ignored in the transition period and fear an even smaller role as plans for a future government take shape. There seems to be little doubt about this. Yet the Turcomans are a sizeable ethnic community in Iraq, and they deserve to have at least the same amount of rights and privileges as accorded to other ethnic groups. On March 8, 2004, the Iraqi Governing Council produced a transitional administrative law designed to benefit only one minority, which makes up about 17 percent of the Iraqi population.

Article 58 of the transitional administrative law, which delineates "Steps to Remedy Injustice," is purposely vague about the future of Kirkuk. It calls for a redress of "the injustice caused by the previous regime's practices in altering the demographic character of certain regions, including Kirkuk." It states that "individuals newly introduced to specific regions and territories may be resettled, may receive compensation from the state, may receive new land from the state near their residence in the governorate from which they came, or may receive compensation for the cost of moving to such areas." The status of contested cities like Kirkuk will be deferred until after the census and a permanent constitution "consistent with the principle of justice, taking into account the will of the people of those territories." This bland language raises more questions than it answers. Does justice require only the restoration of confiscated property, or does it also require the restoration of Kirkuk's demography to the period before Arabisation? Turcoman rights are therefore open to interpretation. The status of their lands and cities is left to the mercy of future manipulations and machinations. The Turcomans held large demonstrations in Baghdad and Tuzhurmatu, including a hunger strike in front of the Coalition Provisional Authority's headquarters in Baghdad.

All stakeholders in the Iraqi equation need to be considered, and all of them should be treated equally fairly. Evidently, that has not happened. Indeed, all the evidence points in a different direction. The Turcomans who have lived in these territories for over a millennium should be recognised as a constituent people of Iraq, and Turkish must be made one of the official languages. A population of at least two million deserves nothing less. Thousands of Turcomans were pushed out of their homes by Saddam Hussein as part of his Arabisation programme, when he sought to move Arabs into Kirkuk and the surrounding area to increase his influence and change the region's ethnic makeup. The Turcomans have repeatedly said that now that Saddam Hussein was gone, they wanted the areas back. The effects of Arabisation and the deportations that took place in Kirkuk should be redressed. Clearly then, the Turcomans must return to their previous homes in that area, while the Kurds and Arabs, who were brought by the authorities into that area at any time since 1957, should return to their original homes.

International law not only specifies the forced and arbitrary transfer of populations as a crime against humanity but also provides for a remedy for the persons victimised by these forced transfers. Persons forcibly transferred from their homes in violation of international standards are entitled to return to their home areas and property, a right known as the right to return. Most international human rights instruments recognise the right to return to one's country. There is no specific provision in international covenants affirming the right of internally displaced persons to return to their places of origin. However, this right, or at least the obligation of states not to impede the return of people to their places of origin, is implied. For example, Article 12 of the International Covenant on Civil and Political Rights recognises the right to choose freely one's own place of residence, which incorporates the right to return to one's home area. In some cases, the right to return to one's former place of residence is also supported by the right to family reunification and to protection of the family.

Numerous resolutions of the UN General Assembly and of the Security Council, as well as several international peace agreements, also recognise the right to return to one's home and property. All these indicate that persons expelled from their homes on ethnic grounds, as the Turcomans have been, have a right to return to their land and homes and receive restitution. As far as the Turcomans are concerned, however, the Coalition Provisional Authority was extremely dilatory about reversing Saddam Hussein's Arabisation of Kirkuk. Many displaced Turcomans have not yet been able to return to their homes. In conjunction with United Nations experts, the Iraqi government should undertake a systematic effort to return displaced Turcomans to their original homes based on the principles that they have the right to (1) return in safety without risk of harassment, intimidation, persecution, or discrimination on account of their ethnic origin; (2) have restored to them property of which they were deprived; and (3) be compensated for property that cannot be restored.

It is extraordinary that there has been so little media coverage of the future of the Turcomans as an often-threatened community. Most media accounts only take note of the interests of Iraq's non-Turcomans. The Turcomans are not familiar abroad and stay out of world media and news headlines. For many in the West, the history of Iraq's Turcomans is largely unknown. These people inside Iraq have been indigenous for 1,200 years. They have been kind of a major part of the Iraqi landscape, and the West never hears about them. The Turcoman component in Iraq cannot rightfully be regarded as insignificant. Yet most regional studies have either overlooked its existence or have referred to it simply in passing. The Turcoman reality of Iraq is all too often neglected, misunderstood, or ignored.

The Turcomans lack the wherewithal and media know-how to attract the world's attention to their plight. The international concern, which the Turcomans should arouse, has only been reflected in the varying responses of Ankara. World capitals can no longer be indifferent to the tragic destiny of this people. Their position in Iraq is most delicate and needs to be watched with the closest attention. The international community must develop a more concrete agenda towards northern Iraq and should devote more of its time to the human rights dimension of the Turcoman situation, especially by establishing human rights monitors in Kirkuk and by publicising more vigorously past and continuing human rights abuses.

What is still badly lacking in northern Iraq is an effective UN presence. The UN at its best can supply the kind of international legitimacy and impartial expert advice that could help guide the disorganised Turcomans and the inexperienced government politicians towards a better, more far-sighted relationship. The case should also be made to the Security Council to appoint a UN special rapporteur to oversee the situation in Kirkuk and report quarterly to the secretary-general on developments and actions that threaten the security and human rights. It is hoped that the fortunes of the Turcomans will attract increasing attention in the world. Surely they deserve more attention than they are given.

Blithely ignoring the presence and rights of one of the main ethno-linguistic components of the Iraqi population will not bring order and sustaining stability to

Iraqis and Iraq but will create chaos and animosity among the entire population. The Turcomans had expected to be included in the Iraqi Governing Council and in the interim government proportionate with their true demographical ratio and represented by their largest political organisation, the Iraqi Turcoman Front. The Turcomans complain that their share of the population is being wilfully underrepresented. They are angry that their urban districts are being preemptively gerrymandered by Kurdish factions to carve out a greater Iraqi Kurdistan in a future bid for oil terrain. In recent years, the Turcomans have not been allowed to declare themselves as anything other than Arab or Kurdish, so the current population figures are dubious in the extreme.

Iraq's constitution has been ratified on October 15, 2005—but by the narrowest of margins. Shiite Arabs and Kurds approved the constitution, with at least 95 percent of the electorate voting yes. The overwhelmingly Sunni Arab Anbar province and the majority Sunni Arab Salaheddin and Nineveh provinces, however, rejected the ballot with 97, 82, and 55 percent voting no, respectively. Yet opportunities still exist to bring the Sunni Arabs and other elements of opposition into the political process. In a last-minute deal aimed at getting the Sunni Arabs on board, the constitutional drafters added a mechanism to review and amend the constitution in the year 2006. Therefore, the constitution is still not the final version.

The present situation in Iraq demands a new approach for the future. For Iraq to become a viable state, the permanent constitution must establish a system of governance that addresses the core concerns of Iraq's diverse communities. The ultimate security of the Iraqi political and social fabric lies in the ability of all groups to reconcile their priorities and interests. People from every group must put their identity as Iraqis ahead of their ethnic or religious affiliations. All communal segments of the country should be represented in political institutions proportionate to their population. They must also assume offices in the state administration commensurate with their size.

The Turcoman community's numbers have been deliberately underestimated in all population counts. As a result, qualified and representative Turcomans have been kept out of key positions in the cabinets and the constitution-drafting process. The Turcomans can undoubtedly be a great asset to Iraq if given the share of representation that is their due. Being industrious and law-abiding subjects, they add a richness and variety to the Iraqi scene and contribute their particular gifts to its society and economics. The Turcomans are a well-educated and skilled community that will be helpful in the country's reconstruction. A new Iraq will hopefully be able to draw extensively on them for its various needs.

As the third largest group of people in Iraq, the Turcomans have become a considerable factor in the country's future stability. The equilibrium in Iraq can best be served by the Turcomans' decision to reassert themselves as a player in shaping Iraq's new order. The building of a democratic Iraq is a great opportunity for the Turcomans to contribute to the country's political, economic, and cultural life as equal partners of other ethnicities without giving up their own Turcoman identity. Yet one cannot construct a modern, liberal, secular, sustainable state capable of reshaping the lives of the Iraqi people if democratic nation-building efforts ignore the Turcoman reality. The international community should take responsibility for ensuring that the Turcomans participate in the restructuring of their country's future. What is needed at this crucial stage is a fair and impartial census in a safe and secure environment, under the monitoring and supervision of the UN Organisation—and soon. It is anticipated that the census will produce the first authentic statistical record of the population of Iraq. However, no definite date has yet been set for the task; and at the time of writing, the scheme seems to be at a standstill.

APPENDIX I

Final Statement of the Meeting of Representatives of Turkey and the United States with the delegations of ADM, CMM, INA, INC, ITF, KDP, PUK and SCIRI (*)
19 March 2003
Ankara, Turkey
(http://www.mfa.gov.tr/grupa/ai/irak/AnkaraMeeting.htm)

REPRESENTATIVES OF TURKEY and the United States met with delegations of ADM, CMM, INA, INC, ITF, KDP, PUK and SCIRI (**) on March 19, 2003, in Ankara, Turkey.

All participants agree that among their principal objectives regarding the future of Iraq are the following:

— Enabling the Iraqi people to build a fully representative and democratic government that meets international standards, including free and fair elections, respect for the rule of law and private property, equality before the law and respect for human rights, consistent with principles agreed at the opposition conference in London.

— Preservation of Iraq's independence, sovereignty, territorial integrity and national unity;

— Elimination of Iraq's weapons of mass destruction capabilities, in accordance with relevant United Nations Security Council resolutions;

— Full compliance with all relevant UNSC resolutions to allow for Iraq's full re-integration into the world community so that there would be no need for sanctions or no-fly zones;

— Determining the future political system and the constitution for Iraq through the full participation and free consent of the totality of the Iraqi population.

— Using the natural resources of Iraq as a national asset and for the Iraqi people as a whole, to strengthen the national economy;

— Making use of the above principal objectives, in order to help foster national unity and reflect the reality that all parts and cities of Iraq belong to the nation as a whole, in perpetuity;

— Protecting civilian lives and property, strongly discouraging the uncontrolled movements of refugees and internally displaced persons, and strongly discouraging Iraqis from taking the law into their own hands or inciting civil discord. All claims will be addressed via a commission that will quickly be set up for a legal and organized process to address the restitution of homes seized previously by the Iraqi regime, and other claims. All Iraqis who have rightful claims will be able to resolve them in a peaceful and orderly manner through this commission;

— Elimination of discrimination based on race, ethnic origin, gender, language or religious conviction. The protection of the rights and freedoms of all constituent peoples of Iraq—Arabs, Kurds, Turkomans, Assyrians, Chaldeans and others—will be paramount in a future Iraq;

— The reformation of the Iraqi national military, to include the reintegration of all militia organizations (including those forces now operating under the command of the Iraqi opposition) and the reformation of Iraq's security institutions;

— Elimination of terrorism and of support for terrorism in and from Iraq, as well as denial of safe havens and weaponry to terrorists.

(*)   Delegations are listed in alphabetical order.
(**)   Abbreviations:
ADM: Assyrian Democratic Movement
CMM: Constitutional Monarchy Movement
INA: Iraqi National Accord
INC: Iraqi National Congress
ITF: Iraqi Turkoman Front
KDP: Kurdistan Democratic Party
PUK: Patriotic Union of Kurdistan
SCIRI: Supreme Council for Islamic Revolution in Iraq

APPENDIX II

Declaration of the Kingdom of Iraq, Made at Baghdad on May 30th, 1932, on the Occasion of the Termination of the Mandatory Regime in Iraq, and Containing the Guarantees Given to the Council by the Iraqi Government

[League of Nations Official Journal, July 1932, Annex 1373, pp.1347-1350.]

Chapter I

Article 1

The stipulations contained in the present chapter are recognised as fundamental laws of Iraq, and no law, regulation or official action shall conflict or interfere with these stipulations, nor shall any law, regulation or official action now or in the future prevail over them.

Article 2

1. Full and complete protection of life and liberty will be assured to all inhabitants of Iraq without distinction of birth, nationality, language, race or religion.
2. All inhabitants of Iraq will be entitled to the free exercise, whether public or private, of any creed, religion or belief, whose practice are not inconsistent with public order or public morals.

Article 3

Ottoman subjects habitually resident in the territory of Iraq on August 6th, 1924, shall be deemed to have acquired on that date Iraqi nationality to the exclusion of Ottoman nationality in accordance with Article 30 of

the Lausanne Peace Treaty and under the conditions laid down in the Iraqi
Nationality Law of October 9th, 1924.

Article 4

1. All Iraqi nationals shall be equal before the law and shall enjoy the same
   civil and political rights without distinction as to race, language or
   religion.
2. The electoral system shall guarantee equitable representation to racial,
   religious and linguistic minorities in Iraq.
3. Differences of race, language or religion shall not prejudice any Iraqi
   national in matters relating to the enjoyment of civil or political rights, as,
   for instance, admission to public employments, functions and honours,
   or the exercise of professions or industries.
4. No restriction will be imposed on the free use by any Iraqi national of any
   language, in private intercourse, in commerce, in religion, in the Press or
   in publications of any kind, or at public meetings.
5. Notwithstanding the establishment by the Iraqi Government of Arabic as
   the official language, and notwithstanding the special arrangements to be
   made by the Iraqi Government, under Article 9 of the present Declaration,
   regarding the use of the Kurdish and Turkish languages, adequate facilities
   will be given to all Iraqi nationals whose mother tongue is not the official
   language, for the use of their language, either orally or in writing, before
   the courts.

Article 5

Iraqi nationals who belong to racial, religious or linguistic minorities
will enjoy the same treatment and security in law and in fact as other Iraqi
nationals. In particular, they shall have an equal right to maintain, manage
and control at their own expense, or to establish in the future, charitable,
religious and social institutions, schools and other educational establishments,
with the right to use their own language and to exercise their religion freely
therein.

Article 6

The Iraqi Government undertakes to take, as regards non-Moslem
minorities, in so far as concerns their family law and personal status, measures

permitting the settlement of these questions in accordance with the customs and usage of the communities to which those minorities belong.

The Iraqi Government will communicate to the Council of the League of Nations information regarding the manner in which these measures have been executed.

Article 7

1. The Iraqi Government undertakes to grant full protection, facilities and authorisation to the churches, synagogues, cemeteries and other religious establishments, charitable works and pious foundations of minority religious communities existing in Iraq.

2. Each of these communities shall have the right of establishing councils, in important administrative districts, competent to administer pious foundations and charitable bequests. These councils shall be competent to deal with the collection of income derived therefrom, and the expenditure thereof in accordance with the wishes of the donor or with the custom in use among the community. These communities shall also undertake the supervision of the property of orphans, in accordance with law. The councils referred to above shall be under the supervision of the Government.

3. The Iraqi Government will not refuse, for the formation of new religious or charitable institutions, any of the necessary facilities which may be guaranteed to existing institutions of that nature.

Article 8

1. In the public educational system in towns and districts in which are resident a considerable proportion of Iraqi nationals whose mother tongue is not the official language, the Iraqi Government will make provision for adequate facilities for ensuring that in the primary schools instruction shall be given to the children of such nationals through the medium of their own language; it being understood that this provision does not prevent the Iraqi Government from making the teaching of Arabic obligatory in the said schools.

2. In towns and districts where there is a considerable proportion of Iraqi nationals belonging to racial, religious or linguistic minorities, these minorities will be assured an equitable share in the enjoyment and application of sums which may be provided out of public funds under the

State, municipal or other budgets for educational, religious or charitable purposes.

Article 9

1. Iraq undertakes that in the liwas of Mosul, Arbil, Kirkuk, and Sulaimaniya, the official language, side by side with Arabic, shall be Kurdish in the qadhas in which the population is predominantly of Kurdish race.

   In the qadhas of Kifri and Kirkuk, however, in the liwa of Kirkuk, where a considerable part of the population is of Turcoman race, the official language, side by side with Arabic, shall be either Kurdish or Turkish.
2. Iraq undertakes that in the said qadhas the officials shall, subject to justifiable exceptions, have a competent knowledge of Kurdish or Turkish as the case may be.
3. Although in these qadhas the criterion for the choice of officials will be, as in the rest of Iraq, efficiency and knowledge of the language, rather than race, Iraq undertakes that the officials shall, as hitherto, be selected, so far as possible, from among Iraqis from one or other of these qadhas.

Article 10

The stipulations of the foregoing articles of this Declaration, so far as they affect persons belonging to racial, religious or linguistic minorities, are declared to constitute obligations of international concern and will be placed under the guarantee of the League of Nations. No modification will be made in them without the assent of a majority of the Council of the League of Nations.

Any Member of the League represented on the Council shall have the right to bring to the attention of the Council any infraction or danger of infraction of any of these stipulations, and the Council may thereupon take such measures and give such directions as it may deem proper and effective in the circumstances.

Any difference of opinion as to questions of law or fact arising out of these articles between Iraq and any Member of the League represented on the Council shall be held to be a dispute of an international character under Article 14 of the Covenant of the League of Nations. Any such dispute shall, if the other party thereto demands, be referred to the Permanent Court of International Justice. The decision of the Permanent Court shall be final and shall have the same force and effect as an award under Article 13 of the Covenant.

Chapter II

Article 11

1. Subject to reciprocity, Iraq undertakes to grant to Members of the League most-favoured-nation treatment for a period of ten years from the date of its admission to membership of the League of Nations.

    Nevertheless, should measures taken by any Member of the League of Nations whether such measures are in force at the above-mentioned date or are taken during the period contemplated in the preceding paragraph, be of such a nature as to disturb to the detriment of Iraq the balance of trade between Iraq and the Member of the League of Nations in question, by seriously affecting the chief exports of Iraq. The latter, in view of its special situation, reserves to itself the right to request the Member of the League of Nations concerned to open negotiations immediately for the purpose of restoring the balance.

    Should an agreement, not be reached by negotiation within three months from its request, Iraq declares that it will consider itself as freed, vis-à-vis of the Member of the League in question, from the obligation laid down in the first sub-paragraph above.

2. The undertaking contained in paragraph 1 above shall not apply to any advantages which are, or may in the future be, accorded by Iraq to any adjacent country in order to facilitate frontier traffic, or to those resulting from a Customs union concluded by Iraq. Nor shall the undertaking apply to any special advantages in Customs matters which Iraq may grant to goods the produce or manufacture of Turkey or of any country whose territory was in 1914 wholly included in the Ottoman Empire in Asia.

Article 12

A uniform system of justice shall be applicable to all, Iraqis and foreigners alike. It shall be such as effectively to ensure the protection and full exercise of their rights both to foreigners and to nationals.

The judicial system at present in force, and based on Articles 2,3 and 4 of the Agreement between the Mandatory Power and Iraq, signed on March 4th, 1931, shall be maintained for a period of 10 years from the date of the admission of Iraq to membership of the League of Nations.

Appointments to the posts reserved for foreign jurists by Article 2 of the said Agreement shall be made by the Iraqi Government. Their holders shall be foreigners, but selected without distinction of nationality; they must be fully qualified.

Article 13

Iraq considers itself bound by all the international agreements and conventions, both general and special, to which it has become a party, whether by its own action or by that of the Mandatory Power acting on its behalf. Subject, to any right of denunciation provided for therein, such agreements and conventions shall be respected by Iraq throughout the period for which they were concluded.

Article 14

Iraq, taking note of the resolution of the Council of the League of Nations of September 15th, 1925:

1. Declares that all rights of whatever nature acquired before the termination of the mandatory regime by individuals, associations or juridical persons shall be respected.
2. Undertakes to respect and fulfil all financial obligations of whatever nature assumed on Iraq's behalf by the Mandatory Power during the period of the Mandate.

Article 15

Subject to such measures as may be essential for the maintenance of public order and morality, Iraq undertakes to ensure and guarantee throughout, its territory freedom of conscience and worship and the free exercise of the religious, educational and medical activities of religious missions of all denominations, whatever the nationality of those missions or of their members.

Article 16

The provisions of the present chapter constitute obligations of international concern. Any Member of the League of Nations may call the attention of the Council to any infraction of these provisions. They may not be modified except by agreement between Iraq and the Council of the League of Nations acting by a majority vote.

Any difference of opinion which may arise between Iraq and any Member of the League of Nations represented on the Council, with regard to the interpretation or the execution of the said provisions, shall, by an application by such Member, be submitted for decision to the Permanent Court of International Justice.

The undersigned, duly authorised, accepts on behalf of Iraq, subject to ratification, the above provisions, being the declaration provided for by the resolution of the Council of the League of Nations of May 19th, 1932.

Done at Baghdad on this thirtieth day of May 1932 in a single copy which shall be deposited in the archives of the Secretariat of the League of Nations.

(Signed) NOURY SA'ID,
Prime Minister of Iraq

BIBLIOGRAPHY

I. Unpublished Primary Sources

A. Official

1) British Library, Euston, London

India Office Records (IO).

2) League of Nations, Geneva

Document No.C.400,M-147, 1925, VII, dated 16 July 1925. "Report submitted to the Council by the Commission instituted by the Council Resolution of 30 September 1924."

3) National Archives, Kew, London

Air Ministry Papers (AIR).
Colonial Office Papers (CO).
Foreign Office Papers (FO).

4) National Archives and Records Administration, Washington DC.

Department of State Papers (USNA).

B. Private

1) Middle Eastern Centre, St. Antony's College, Oxford

Cecil John Edmonds Papers.
Reader Bullard Papers.

William Rupert Hay Papers.

II. Published Primary Sources

A. Official

1) Britain:

Admiralty. Naval Staff. Geographical Section of the Naval Intelligence Division. *A Handbook of Iraq and the Persian Gulf.* London: His Majesty's Stationery Office, 1944.

Command Papers, 1920-1939.

Documents on British Foreign Policy, Series 1, 1919-1939. Llewellyn Woodward and Rohan Butler, ed., London: Her Majesty's Stationery Office, 1960.

Foreign Office. Historical Section, No. 63. *Mesopotamia*, London: His Majesty's Stationery Office, 1920.

Great Britain. Treaty Series, 1920-1939.

2) European Parliament:

Document No.P5-TA (2002) 0248, dated 16 May 2002. "Resolution on the situation in Iraq eleven years after the Gulf war."

3) League of Nations:

Minutes of the Permanent Mandates Commission, 1921-1939.
Official Journal, 1920-1939.
Treaty Series, 1920-1939.

4) Turkey:

Atatürk'ün Söylev ve Demeçleri (Atatürk's Speeches and Statements). Ankara: Atatürk Kültür, Dil ve Tarih Yüksek Kurumu, 1989.

Cumhuriyetin İlk On Yılı ve Balkan Paktı 1923-1934 (The First Ten Years of the Republic and the Balkan Pact 1923-1934). Ankara: T. C. Dışişleri Bakanlığı, 1973.

Nutuk (Speech). Ankara: Atatürk Kültür, Dil ve Tarih Yüksek Kurumu, 1989.

Türkiye Büyük Millet Meclisi Tutanak Dergisi (The Minutes of Proceedings of the Turkish Grand National Assembly). Ankara: Türkiye Büyük Millet Meclisi, 1920-2004.

5) United Nations:

Economic and Social Council. Commission on Human Rights. Forty-eighth session, agenda item 12, Document No. E/CN.4/1992/31, dated 18 February 1992. "Report on the situation of human rights in Iraq prepared by the special rapporteur Max van der Stoel in accordance with Commission resolution 1991/74."

Economic and Social Council. Commission on Human Rights. Forty-ninth session, agenda item 12, Document No. E/CN.4/1993/45, dated 19 February 1993. "Report on the situation of human rights in Iraq prepared by the special rapporteur Max van der Stoel in accordance with Commission resolution 1992/71."

Economic and Social Council. Commission on Human Rights. Fiftieth session, agenda item 12, Document No. E/CN.4/1994/58, dated 25 February 1994. "Report on the situation of human rights in Iraq submitted by the special rapporteur Max van der Stoel in accordance with Commission resolution 1993/74."

Economic and Social Council. Commission on Human Rights. Fifty-fifth session, agenda item 9, Document No. E/CN.4/1999/37, dated 26 February 1999. "Report on the situation of human rights in Iraq submitted by the special rapporteur Max van der Stoel in accordance with Commission resolution 1998/65."

Economic and Social Council. Commission on Human Rights. Sixty-first session, item 6 (a) of the provisional agenda, Document No. E/CN.4/2005/ NGO/261, dated 10 March 2005. Written statement entitled "Racism, racial discrimination, xenophobia, and all forms of discrimination: comprehensive implementation of and follow-up to the Durban Declaration and Programme of Action" submitted by the Transnational Radical Party.

General Assembly. Forty-sixth session, agenda item 98 (c), Document No. A/46/647, dated 13 November 1991. "Situation of human rights in Iraq: Note by the Secretary-General."

General Assembly. Fifty-first session, agenda item 110 (c), Document No. A/51/496/Add.1, dated 8 November 1996. "Situation of human rights in Iraq: Note by the Secretary-General."

General Assembly. Fifty-first session, agenda item 110 (c), Document No. A/52/476/Add.1, dated 15 October 1997. "Situation of human rights in Iraq: Note by the Secretary-General."

General Assembly. Commission on Human Rights. Fifty-first session, agenda item 10, Document No. E/CN.4/1987/67, dated 10 March 1998. "Report on the violations of human rights in Iraq submitted by the special rapporteur Max van der Stoel in accordance with Commission resolution 1997/60."

Treaty Series, 1945-2004.

Yearbook of the United Nations 1946-1947. United Nations, Lake Success, NY: Department of Public Information, 1947.

6) United States:

Foreign Relations of the United States. Diplomatic Papers (1958-1960). Washington DC: State Department, 1993.

Papers Relating to the Foreign Affairs of the United States. The Paris Peace Conference, 1919. Washington DC: United States Government Printing Office, 1943.

B. Private (Memoirs, correspondences, statements, contemporary studies)

Bowman, Humphrey. *Middle East Window.* London: Longmans, Green and Co., 1942.

Bullard, Reader. *The Camels Must Go.* London: Faber and Faber, 1961.

Edmonds, Cecil John. *Kurds, Turks and Arabs: Politics, Travel and Research in North-Eastern Iraq 1919-1925.* London: Oxford University Press, 1957.

Fieldhouse, D. K., ed. *Kurds, Arabs and Britons: The Memoir of Wallace Lyon in Iraq, 1910-1941.* London: I. B. Tauris, 2002.

Hay, William Rupert. *Two Years in Kurdistan: Experiences of a Political Officer, 1918-1920.* London: Sidgwick and Jackson, 1921.

Tepeyran, Ebubekir Hazım. *Hatıralar* (Recollections). 2nd ed. İstanbul: Pera Turizm ve Ticaret, 1998.

Toynbee, Arnold, ed. *Survey of International Affairs* (1934). London: Oxford University Press, 1935.

Trevelyan, Humphrey. *The Middle East in Revolution.* London: MacMillan, 1970.

Wilson, Arnold. *Mesopotamia 1917-1920: A Clash of Loyalties.* London: Oxford University Press, 1931.

III. Newspapers

English: *Chicago Tribune* (Chicago), *Financial Times* (London), *International Herald Tribune* (New York), *Los Angeles Times* (Los Angeles), *South Florida Sun-Sentinel* (Florida), *The Daily Telegraph* (London), *The Guardian* (London), *The New York Times* (New York), *The Times* (London), *The Wall Street Journal* (New York), *The Washington Post* (Washington), *Turkish Daily News* (Ankara).

French: *Le Monde* (Paris).

Turkish: *Akşam* (İstanbul), *Cumhuriyet* (İstanbul), *Halka ve Olaylara Tercüman* (İstanbul), *Hürriyet* (İstanbul), *Milliyet* (İstanbul), *Ortadoğu* (İstanbul), *Radikal* (İstanbul), *Sabah* (İstanbul), *Türkiye* (İstanbul), *Vakit* (İstanbul), *Vatan* (İstanbul), *Yeniçağ* (İstanbul), *Yeni Şafak* (İstanbul), *Zaman* (İstanbul).

IV. Secondary Sources

A. Books

Aburish, Said. *Saddam Hussein: The Politics of Revenge*. London: Bloomsburry, 2000.

Batatu, Hanna. *The Old Social Classes and the Revolutionary Movements of Iraq: A Study of Iraq's Old Landed and Commercial Classes and of Its Communists, Baathists, and Free Officers*. Princeton, NJ: Princeton University Press, 1978.

Bodansky, Yossef. *The Secret History of the Iraq War*. New York: Harper Collins, 2004.

Catherwood, Christopher. *Winston's Folly*. London: Constable and Robinson, 2004.

Dodge, Toby. *Inventing Iraq: The Failure of Nation Building and a History Denied*. New York: Columbia University Press, 2003.

Farouk-Sluglett, Marion, and Peter Sluglett. *Iraq since 1958: From Revolution to Dictatorship*. London: I. B. Tauris, 1990.

Foster, Henry. *The Making of Modern Iraq*. Norman, OK: University of Oklahoma Press, 1935.

Fuccaro, Nelida. *The Other Kurds: Yazidis in Colonial Iraq*. London: I. B. Tauris, 1999.

Gönlübol, Mehmet, and Cem Sar. *Olaylarla Türk Dış Politikası 1919-1965* (Turkish Foreign Policy Through Events 1919-1965). Ankara: Dışişleri Bakanlığı Matbaası, 1968.

Graham-Brown, Sarah. *Sanctioning Saddam: The Politics of Intervention in Iraq*. London: I. B. Tauris, 1999.

Güçlü, Yücel. *The Question of the Sanjak of Alexandretta: A Study in Turkish-French-Syrian Relations*. Ankara: Türk Tarih Kurumu Basımevi, 2001.

Hale, William. *Turkish Foreign Policy 1774-2000*. London: Frank Cass, 2000.

Hurewitz, J. C., ed. *Diplomacy in the Near and Middle East: A Documentary Record 1914-1956*, vol. 2. Princeton, NJ: Van Nostrand, 1956.

Hürmüzlü, Erşat. *Türkmenler ve Irak* (Turcomans and Iraq). İstanbul: Kerkük Vakfi, 2003.

Irak Türkleri Bibliyografyası (A Bibliography of Iraqi Turks). Ankara: T. C. Başbakanlık Devlet Arşivleri Genel Müdürlüğü, 1994.

Ireland, Philip Willard. *Iraq: A Study in Political Development*. London: Jonathan Cape, 1937.

Keay, John. *Sowing the Wind: The Seeds of Conflict in the Middle East*. London: John Murray, 2003.

Khadduri, Majid. *Republican Iraq: A Study in Iraqi Politics since the Revolution of 1958*. London: Oxford University Press, 1969.

Kirk, George. *Contemporary Arab Politics: A Concise History*. New York: Frederick Praeger, 1961.

Küzeci, Şemsettin. *Kerkük Soykırımları (Kirkuk Genocides)*. Ankara: Teknoed Yayınları, 2004.

Longrigg, Stephen Hemsley. *Four Centuries of Modern Iraq*. Oxford: Oxford University Press, 1925.

—. *Iraq, 1900 to 1950: A Political, Social, And Economic History*. 2nd ed. London: Oxford University Press, 1956.

—. *The Middle East: A Social Geography*. Chicago, IL: Aldine, 1963.

Longrigg, Stephen Hemsley, and Frank Stoakes. *Iraq*. London: Ernest Benn, 1958.

Lukitz, Liora. *Iraq: The Search for National Identity*. London: Frank Cass, 1995.

Main, Ernest. *Iraq From Mandate to Independence*. London: George Allen and Unwin, 1935.

Mango, Andrew. *Atatürk*. London: John Murray, 1999.

Marr, Phebe. *The Modern History of Iraq*. Boulder, CO: Westview Press, 1985.

Marufoğlu, Sinan. *Osmanlı Döneminde Kuzey Irak* (Northern Iraq in Ottoman Era). İstanbul: Eren Yayıncılık, 1998.

McDowall, David. *A Modern History of the Kurds*. London: I. B. Tauris, 1996.

Mejcher, Helmut. *Imperial Quest for Oil: Iraq 1910-1928*. London: Ithaca Press, 1976.

Nyrop, Richard. *Area Handbook for Iraq*. Washington DC: United States Government Printing House, 1971.

Oates, David. *Studies in the Ancient History of Northern Iraq*. London: Oxford University Press, 1968.

O'Ballance, Edgar. *The Kurdish Struggle, 1920-1994*. London: MacMillan, 1996.

Oran, Baskın, ed. *Türk Dış Politikası 1919-1980* (Turkish Foreign Policy 1919-1980), vol.1. İstanbul: İletişim Yayınları, 2001.

Saatçı, Suphi. *Kerkük Evleri* (Kirkuk Houses). İstanbul: Klasik Yayınevi, 2003.

——. *Tarihi Gelişim İçinde Irak'ta Türk Varlığı* (Turkish Existence in Iraq Within Historical Development). İstanbul: Tarihi Araştırmalar ve Dokümantasyon Merkezleri Kurma ve Geliştirme Vakfı, 1996.

——. *Tarihten Günümüze Irak Türkmenleri* (Iraqi Turcomans from History to Our Day). İstanbul: Ötüken Neşriyat, 2003.

Sander, Oral. *Siyasi Tarih 1918-1994* (Political History 1918-1994). Ankara: İmge Kitabevi, 2004.

Silverfarb, Daniel. *Britain's Informal Empire in the Middle East: A Case Study of Iraq, 1929-1941.* New York: Oxford University Press, 1986.

Sluglett, Peter. *Britain in Iraq 1914-1932.* London: Ithaca Press, 1976.

Stafford, R. S. *The Tragedy of the Assyrian Minority in Iraq.* London: Kegan Paul, 2004.

Starr, Richard. *Nuzi,* vol.1. Cambridge, MA: Harvard University Press, 1939.

Stivers, William. *Supremacy and Oil: Iraq, Turkey, and the Anglo-American World Order 1918-1930.* Ithaca, NY: Cornell University Press, 1982.

Taylor, Scott. *Among The 'Others': Encounters with the Forgotten Turkmen of Iraq.* Ottawa: Esprit De Corps Books, 2004.

——. *Spinning on the Axis of Evil: America's War Against Iraq.* Ottawa: Esprit De Corps Books, 2003.

Tripp, Charles. *A History of Iraq.* Cambridge: Cambridge University Press, 2000.

Uluğbay, Hikmet. *İmparatorluktan Cumhuriyete Petropolitik* (Petropolitics from Empire to Republic). Ankara: Turkish Daily News Yayınları, 1995.

Winstone, H. V. F. *Gertrude Bell: A Biography*. London: Constable, 1993.

Yakupoğlu, Enver. *Irak Türkleri* (Iraqi Turks). İstanbul: Boğaziçi Yayınları, 1976.

Yenerer, Vedat. *Düşman Kardeşler: ABD İşgalindeki Irak'ta Arap, Kürt ve Türkmen Çatışması* (Hostile Brethren: Arab, Kurdish and Turcoman Clash in Iraq under US Occupation). İstanbul: Bulut Yayınları, 2004.

Zürcher, Erik. *Turkey: A Modern History.* London: I. B. Tauris, 1993.

B. Articles

Ateş, Sönmez. "Irak Türkleri Hakkında" [On Iraqi Turks]. *Türk Kültürü*, vol. 1, no. 5 (March 1963).

—. "Irak Türkleri İle İlgili Yayınlar Hakkında Düşünceler" [Reflections on Publications about Iraqi Turcomans]. *Türk Kültürü*, vol. 3, no. 25 (November 1964).

Benderoğlu, Abdüllatif. "Irak Türkmen Edebiyatında Şiir, Hikaye ve Roman" [Poem, Story and Novel in the Iraqi Turcoman Literature]. *Türk Kültürü*, vol. 34, no. 394 (February 1996).

Cox, Jafna. "A Splendid Training Ground: The Importance to the Royal Air Force of its Role in Iraq 1919-1932." *Journal of Imperial and Commonwealth History*, vol. 13, no. 2 (January 1985).

Demirci, Fazıl. "Irak'taki Demografik ve Etnik Yapı İçerisinde Irak Türkleri" [Iraqi Turks Within the Demographic and Ethnic Structure in Iraq]. *Türk Kültürü*, vol. 30, no. 359 (March 1993).

—. "Irak Türklerinin Bugünkü Yerleşim Yerleri" [The Present Areas of Settlement of the Iraqi Turcomans]. *Kerkük*, vol. 1, no. 1 (January 1991).

Dobbs, Henry. "Mosul Oil and the Pipe-Line." *Nineteenth Century and After*, vol. 108, no. 643 (September 1930).

Edmonds, Cecil John. "The Kurds and Revolution in Iraq." *Middle East Journal*, vol. 13, no. 1 (Winter 1959).

—. "The Kurds of Iraq." *Middle East Journal*, vol. 11, no. 2 (Winter 1957).

Esin, Necmettin. "Irak Türkleri I" [Iraqi Turks I]. *Türk Kültürü*, vol. 1, no. 1 (November 1962).

—. "Irak Türkleri Edebiyatından Yapraklar" [Leaves from the Literature of Iraqi Turks]. *Türk Kültürü*, vol. 11, no. 123 (January 1973).

—. "Irak Türklerinin Maarifine ve Genel Kültürüne Toplu Bir Bakış" [An Overview of the Education and General Culture of Iraqi Turks]. *Türk Kültürü*, vol. 2, no. 18 (April 1964).

—. "Irak Türkleri ve Musul Meselesi" [Iraqi Turks and the Mosul Question]. *Türk Kültürü*, vol. 12, nos. 139-141 (May/June/July 1974).

—. "Tarihi Bir Türk Şehri: Kerkük" [A Historic Turkish City: Kirkuk]. *Türk Kültürü*, vol. 12, no. 135 (January 1974).

Farouk-Sluglett, Marion, and Peter Sluglett. "The Historiography of Modern Iraq." *American Historical Review*, vol. 96, no. 5 (December 1991).

Foreign Affairs. "The Iraq Dispute: Note and Map", vol. 3, no. 4 (July 1925).

Gandy, Christopher. "The Case of the Kurdish Agha: Vice-Consul Hony in Mosul 1911-1913." *Asian Affairs*, vol. 18, no. 2 (June 1987).

Gorvett, Jon. "Turcoman Trouble Causes Anxiety in Ankara." *Middle East*, vol. 31, no. 350 (November 2004).

Güçlü, Yücel. "Iraq on the Way to Its New Constitution: The Ottoman Experience and Turkish Example." *International Journal of Turkish Studies*, vol. 11, nos. 1 and 2 (Fall 2005).

—. "The Basic Principles and Practices of the Turkish Foreign Policy Under Atatürk." *Belleten*, vol. 114, no. 241 (December 2000).

—. "The Role of the Ottoman-Trained Officers in Independent Iraq." *Oriente Moderno*, vol. 21 (132), no. 2 (December 2002).

Kafesoğlu, İbrahim. "Türkmen Adı, Manası ve Mahiyeti" [The Name, Meaning and Nature of Turcoman]. *Kardaşlık*, vol. 10, nos. 7-8 (November-December 1971).

Kalafat, Yaşar. "Kerkük Yöresi Türkmenleri ve Türkmen Halk İnançları" [Turcomans of Kirkuk Region and Turcoman Popular Beliefs]. *Türk Dünyası Araştırmaları*, vol. 21, no. 417 (January 1998).

Karsh, Efraim. "Reactive Imperialism: Britain, the Hashemites, and the Creation of Modern Iraq." *Journal of Imperial and Commonwealth History*, vol. 30, no. 3 (September 2002).

Ketene, Cengiz. "Kerkük'ün Müstesna Siması Ata Terzibaşı" [The Exceptional Figure of Kirkuk Ata Terzibaşı]. *Türk Kültürü*, vol. 31, no. 359 (March 1993).

Luft, Gal. "Reconstructing Iraq: Bringing Iraq's Economy Back Online." *Middle East Quarterly*, vol. 12, no. 3 (Summer 2005).

Middle East Economic Digest "ENKA to Expand Turkey Pipeline," vol. 27, no. 11(18-24 March 1983).

Middle East Economic Digest "New Pipeline Ups Oil Export Capacity," vol. 31, no. 31(1-7 August 1987).

Middle East Economic Digest "Oil Pipeline Through Turkey Agreed," vol. 17, no. 35 (31 August 1973).

Middle East Economic Survey "Further Delay to Iraq's Northern Crude Exports Resumption," vol. 158, no. 14 (4 April 2005).

Middle East Economic Survey "Gulfsands Signs Misan Gas Project Memorandum of Understanding," vol. 158, no. 8 (21 February 2005).

Middle East Economic Survey "Heritage Oil Joins List of International Oil Companies Pursuing Ventures in Iraqi Kurdistan," vol. 157, nos. 5152 (20 December 2004).

Middle East Economic Survey "Iraq Warns International Oil Companies Against Circumventing Central Government in Oil Talks," vol. 157, no.29 (19 July 2004).

Middle East Economic Survey "Iraqi Crude Quality Declining," vol. 158, no. 27 (4 July 2005).

Middle East Economic Survey "Iraqi Insurgents Target Domestic Energy Supplies," vol. 157, no. 47 (22 November 2004).

Middle East Economic Survey "Iraqi Kurds Demand Right to Own and Manage Northern Oil Reserves," vol. 157, no. 24 (14 June 2004).

Middle East Economic Survey "Northern Challenge," vol. 157, no. 41 (11 October 2004).

Middle East Economic Survey "Revenue from Future Iraqi Kurdistan Oil Finds Must Be for Kurds, Says Barzani. DNO Accord," vol. 157, no. 27 (5 July 2004).

Middle East Economic Survey "Sabotage Derails SOMO's Efforts to Sell Kirkuk on Term Basis," vol. 157, no. 36 (6 September 2004).

Middle East Economic Survey "State Organisation for Marketing of Oil Makes Partial Award of Four Million Barrel Kirkuk Tender," vol. 158, no. 27 (4 July 2005).

Middle East Economic Survey "Talks Start on Suba and Luhais Oil Field Development Contracts," vol. 157, no. 48 (29 November 2004).

Oğuzlu, Tarık. "Endangered Community: The Turkoman Identity in Iraq." *Journal of Muslim Minority Affairs,* vol. 24, no. 2 (October 2004).

—. "The Turkomans as a Factor in Turkish Foreign Policy." *Turkish Studies,* vol. 3, no. 2 (Autumn 2002).

Omissi, David. "Britain, the Assyrians and the Iraq Levies, 1919-1932." *Journal of Imperial and Commonwealth History,* vol. 17, no. 3 (September 1989).

Rubin, Michael. Review of *Among the 'Others': Encounters with the Forgotten Turkmen of Iraq. Middle East Quarterly*, vol. 12, no. 3 (Summer 2005).

Sümer, Faruk. "Irak Türklerinin Tarihine Kısa Bir Bakış" [A Brief Glance at the History of Iraqi Turks]. *Türk Kültürü*, vol. 15, no. 180 (October 1977).

Vesely, Milan. "Iraq's Oil Wealth Fuel Fires of Discontent." *Middle East*, vol. 30, no. 351 (December 2004).

Williams, Kenneth. "The Significance of Mosul." *Nineteenth Century and After*, vol. 99, no. 589 (March 1926).

Williams, Wilbur. "The State of Iraq: A Mandate Attains Independence." *Foreign Policy Report*, vol. 18, no. 16 (12 October 1932).

Wilson, Arnold. "The Crisis in Iraq." *Nineteenth Century and After*, vol. 114, no. 680 (October 1933).

Wright, Quincy. "The Mosul Dispute." *American Journal of International Law*, vol. 20, no. 3 (July 1926).

ENDNOTES

1   As used in this text, *Turcomans* refers to the Turcomans of Iraq unless otherwise mentioned.

2   The term *Middle East* is variously defined. In this work it covers Turkey, the Levant, Mesopotamia, Arabia, the Persian Gulf, and Iran.

3   Although the communal dimension in the development of Iraqi politics and society is generally acknowledged, western scholars have not paid much attention to Turcomans; and none has given more than a few passing pages to the matters under discussion here. Indeed, in several relevant works they are omitted altogether. Therefore, social science literature on Iraqi Turcomans in western languages is negligible. Contemporary scholarship in this field has lagged behind lamentably. A weakness of many works on Iraq, whether they are of a reference or an analytical nature, is that they fail to refer adequately to, or include analyses of, Turcomans. Recent historiography has overlooked their importance. For literature in English on Iraq, from the origins of the modern state up to 1991, see in particular the review article by Marion Farouk-Sluglett and Peter Sluglett, "The Historiography of Modern Iraq," *The American Historical Review*, vol. 96, no. 5 (December 1991): 1408-1421. For literature in Turkish on Iraqi Turcomans up to 1994, see *Irak Türkleri Bibliyografyası* [A Bibliography of Iraqi Turks] (Ankara: T. C. Başbakanlık Devlet Arşivleri Genel Müdürlüğü, 1994).

4   Scott Taylor, *Among the 'Others': Encounters with the Forgotten Turkmen of Iraq* (Ottawa: Esprit De Corps Books, 2004), 8. Taylor stands out as a pioneer among those rare Western authors who have shown appreciable understanding of Iraqi Turcomans. He makes his primary home in Ottawa and travels extensively to the Middle East and around the world. *Among the 'Others'* is based on the author's personal experiences and observations gathered during twenty separate trips into Iraq—before and after the toppling of the Baathi regime. The book provides a rare insight into the plight of the Iraqi people.

5   Michael Rubin, "Review of *Among the 'Others': Encounters with the Forgotten Turkmen of Iraq*," *Middle East Quarterly*, vol. 12, no. 3 (Summer 2005): 87.

6   Tarık Oğuzlu, "The Turkomans as a Factor in Turkish Foreign Policy," *Turkish Studies*, vol. 3, no. 2 (Autumn 2002): 139-148 and, by the same author, "Endangered Community: The Turkoman Identity in Iraq," *Journal of Muslim Minority Affairs*, vol. 24, no. 2 (October 2004): 309-325.

7   Richard Nyrop, and others, *Area Handbook for Iraq*, second printing (Washington DC: United States Government Printing House, 1971), 6.

8   For more details on the subject, see http://turkmencephesi.org. All translations from Turkish are my own.

9   In this connection, see the excellent article by İbrahim Kafesoğlu, "Türkmen Adı, Manası ve Mahiyeti" [The Name, Meaning and Nature of Turcoman], *Kardaşlık*, vol. 10, nos. 7-8 (November-December 1971): 18-19. Throughout this text, *Turk* and *Turcoman* are used interchangeably. Context indicates when specific reference is made to the Turks of Turkey.

10   Further historical background information on Iraqi Turcomans can be found in Suphi Saatçi, *Tarihten Günümüze Irak Türkmenleri* [Iraqi Turcomans from History to Our Day] (İstanbul: Ötüken Neşriyat, 2003), 15-79. The author, a native of Kirkuk—already in high sstanding in his world of north Iraqi firsthand observation, reporting, commenting, and up-to-date historical writing—also evaluates Turco-Iraqi relations from a Turcoman perspective on pp. 209-276. See also his *Tarihi Gelişim İçinde Irak'ta Türk Varlığı* [Turkish Existence in Iraq Within Historical Development] (İstanbul: Tarihi Araştırmalar ve Dokümantasyon Merkezleri Kurma ve Geliştirme Vakfı, 1996). Both tomes provide substantive coverage of evolutions of many centuries. These works are clearly the best available on the subject and merit the close attention of any serious, disinterested scholar. It is to be hoped that full English translations of them will be published at an early date. Unfortunately far too little notice is taken of Saatçi's studies by Western commentators.

11   Faruk Sümer, "Irak Türklerinin Tarihine Kısa Bir Bakış" [A Brief Glance at the History of Iraqi Turks], *Türk Kültürü*, vol. 15, no. 180 (October 1977), 44-50.

12   Richard Starr, *Nuzi*, vol. 1 (Cambridge, Mass.: Harvard University Press, 1939), xxxi.

13   For a useful succinct overview, Enver Yakuboğlu, *Irak Türkleri* [Iraqi Turks] (İstanbul: Boğaziçi Yayınları, 1976), 51-63. Also see the interview with Faruk Abdullah Abdurrahman, chairman of the Iraqi Turcoman Front between September 2003 and April 2005, in Vedat Yenerer's work *Düşman Kardeşler: ABD İşgalindeki Irak'ta Arap, Kürt ve Türkmen Çatışması* [Hostile Brethren: Arab, Kurdish and Turcoman Clash in Iraq under US Occupation] (İstanbul: Bulut Yayınları, 2004), 176-183. Over the past sixteen years, Yenerer has

penned numerous inside reports from Iraq—in the process often challenging the conventional wisdom and biases of mass media reports.

[14] Fazıl Demirci, "Irak Türklerinin Bugünkü Yerleşim Yerleri" [The Present Areas of Settlement of the Iraqi Turks], *Kerkük*, vol. 1, no. 1 (January 1991): 4-8.

[15] This is forcefully argued by Melik Kaylan in "Iraq's Bosnians: The Turcomans as Ethnic Scapegoats," *Wall Street Journal*, 30 December 2002, 10.

[16] Lausanne Conference on Near Eastern Affairs 1922-1923. *Records of Proceedings and Draft Terms of Peace*. Command Papers 1814 (London: His Majesty's Stationery Office, 1923) henceforth referred to as the Lausanne Conference Records. Correspondence between Lord Curzon and Ismet Pasha respecting Mosul. Enclosure in Document B. Turkish reply to the British memorandum regarding the Mosul question, p. 374. It should be worth noting here that "the Turks of Iraq spoke a dialect of Western Turkish which was hardly distinguishable from Osmanlı." *Survey of International Affairs* (1934), ed. Arnold Toynbee (London: Oxford University Press, 1935), 117.

[17] Stephen Hemsley Longrigg, *The Middle East: A Social Geography* (Chicago, Ill,: Aldine, 1963), 115-116.

[18] Erşat Hürmüzlü, *Türkmenler ve Irak* [Turcomans and Iraq] (İstanbul: Kerkük Vakfi, 2003), 81-84. This erudite study provides possibly the best contemporary empirical analysis in Turkish of Iraqi Turcoman demographics. The author provides sound judgement, original Arabic source material, and a lifetime of firsthand experience and knowledge. Hürmüzlü's book is also translated into English and Arabic.

[19] Yossef Bodansky, *The Secret History of the Iraq War* (New York: Harper Collins, 2004), 30.

[20] "Kirkuk Isn't Kurdish," Review and Outlook, *Wall Street Journal*, 13 January 2004, 8.

[21] Milan Vesely, "Iraq's Oil Wealth Fuel Fires of Discontent," *Middle East*, vol. 30, no. 351 (December 2004): 26.

[22] See United States Department of State Papers, National Administration of Archives and Records, Washington DC (henceforth referred to as USNA) 890G/6363T84. Oil gusher at Baba Gurgur. John Randolph (Baghdad) to secretary of state, 31 October 1927.

[23] Gal Luft, "Reconstructing Iraq: Bringing Iraq's Economy Back Online," *Middle East Quarterly*, vol. 12, no. 3 (Summer 2005): 25-26.

[24] Ibid., 26

[25] "Iraqi Crude Quality Declining," *Middle East Economic Survey*, vol. 158, no. 27 (4 July 2005): 14.

26 USNA 890G/6363/122. Kirkuk oil fields. Memorandum (Paul Knabenshue),
    16 March 1933.

27 USNA 890G/6363T84/601. Alexandretta and oil. E.A.Y. (Paris) to secretary
    of state, 27 January 1937.

28 See Foreign Office Papers, National Archives, Kew, London (henceforth referred
    to as FO) 371 S1171/22. Pipeline through Turkey. Minute (Paul Gore-Booth),
    21 January 1957. According to unpublished British records, Turkish minister
    of foreign affairs Tevfik Rüştü—in a conversation with British ambassador to
    Ankara, Ronald Lindsay, during the negotiations over the Mosul question on
    6 May 1926—said that the Turkish government had already received proposals
    from some oil companies for constructing a pipeline traversing Turkish territory
    and coming out at İskenderun or Yumurtalık. See FO 371 E2859/62/65.
    Negotiations over Mosul. Ronald Lindsay (Ankara) to FO, 7 May 1926. All
    quotations from British crown copyright documents in the National Archives
    and the British Library, India Office collections, are reproduced by kind
    permission of the controller of Her Majesty's Stationery Office.

29 "Oil Pipeline Through Turkey Agreed," *Middle East Economic Digest*, vol. 17,
    no. 35 (31 August 1973): 1005.

30 Ibid., 1005 and 1013.

31 "ENKA to Expand Turkey Pipeline," *Middle East Economic Digest*, vol. 27, no.
    11 (18--24 March 1983): 19.

32 "New Pipeline Ups Oil Export Capacity," *Middle East Economic Digest*, vol.
    31, no. 31 (1-7 August 1987): 11.

33 In this context, it is instructive to point out that for the territory of northern
    Iraq, there are, owing to the configuration of land and sea, only two conceivable
    natural outlets to markets abroad. One of these is on the Persian Gulf, the
    other either on or close to the Gulf of İskenderun. It must be borne in mind
    that to reach European ports, the Gulf of İskenderun offers a shorter voyage
    than that from the Persian Gulf by nearly four thousand miles and also saves
    the Suez Canal dues. The biggest market for Kirkuk crude is Europe. On the
    importance of the Gulf of İskenderun for northern Iraq see Yücel Güçlü, *The
    Question of the Sanjak of Alexandretta: A Study in Turkish-French-Syrian Relations*
    (Ankara: Türk Tarih Kurumu Basımevi, 2001), 14-15.

34 *Economist Intelligence Unit*, Turkey: Country Profile Report 2004, 51-52.

35 "Sabotage Derails SOMO's Efforts to Sell Kirkuk on Term Basis", *Middle East
    Economic Survey*, vol. 157, no. 36 (6 September 2004): A12.

36 Reuters News Agency, 2 November 2004.

37 Reuters News Agency, 9 November 2004.

38   "Iraqi Insurgents Target Domestic Energy Supplies," *Middle East Economic Survey*, vol. 157, no. 47 (22 November 2004): A3.

39   "Talks Start on Suba and Luhais Oil Field Development Contracts," *Middle East Economic Survey*, vol. 157, no. 48 (29 November 2004): A12.

40   Reuters News Agency, 3 January 2005.

41   "Gulfsands Signs Misan Gas Project Memorandum of Understanding," *Middle East Economic Survey*, vol. 158, no. 8 (21 February 2005): 15.

42   "Further Delay to Iraq's Northern Crude Exports Resumption," *Middle East Economic Survey*, vol. 158, no. 14 (4 April 2005): 15.

43   Chip Cummins and Hasan Hafidh, "Iraq Oil Industry Pumps Away," *Wall Street Journal*, 29 November 2004, A2 and Associated Press News Agency, 30 November 2004.

44   Vesely (2004), 26-27.

45   Luft (2005), 31.

46   "State Organisation for Marketing of Oil Makes Partial Award of Four Million Barrel Kirkuk Tender," *Middle East Economic Survey*, vol. 158, no. 27 (4 July 2005): 14

47   James Glanz, "Thanks to Guards, Iraq Oil Pipeline Is Up and Running On and Off," *New York Times*, 3 September 2005, A6.

48   Luft (2005), 29-30.

49   Text of the final statement of the Ankara meeting of the Iraqi opposition of 19 March 2003 will be found in Appendix I.

50   Rajiv Chandrasekaran and Anthony Shadid, "Iraq's Divided People. Religious and Ethnic Tensions Over Land and Power Are Deepening," *Washington Post National Weekly Edition*, 26-30 October 2003, 8. Also Jeffrey Fleishman, "Kurds Bask in the Fall of Kirkuk; Some Arabs Fear Retribution," *Los Angeles Times*, 11 April 2003, A7.

51   C. J. Chivers, "Kirkuk's Swift Collapse Leaves a City in Chaos," *New York Times*, 11 April 2003, B1, and, by the same correspondent, "A Nation at War: In the Field Special Forces," *New York Times*, 12 April 2003, B1.

52   Karl Vick and Steve Vogel, "Kurds' Looting Sweeps Across Liberated Kirkuk," *Washington Post*, 12 April 2003, A23.

53   C. J. Chivers, "Groups of Kurds Are Driving Arabs From Northern Villages," *New York Times*, 14 April 2003, B1.

54   C. J. Chivers, "Shaky Ground Is Ahead and Behind in the North," *New York Times*, 12 April 2003, B1.

55   C. J. Chivers, "Oil Fields in a Sorry State, Stripped Even of the Toilets," *New York Times*, 20 April 2003, B2.

56   Karl Vick, "Looters Halt Flow of Oil From Kirkuk; Managers Blame United States For Not Stopping Kurds," *Washington Post*, 17 April 2003, A25.

57   Taylor (2004), 118. For Kurds' destruction of the land records at the Kirkuk courthouse, a step that could make it easier for them to force the Turcomans to leave the city, see for instance Steve Vogel, "United States Forces Unopposed in Kirkuk; Troops Greeted by Cheering Crowds," *Washington Post*, 11 April 2003, A36 and Richard Boudreaux, "Powell Reassures Turkey That Armed Kurds Will Leave Kirkuk," *Los Angeles Times*, 11 April 2003, A10. For Turkish press comments on the incident, see for example "Tapuları Siliyorlar" [They Are Destroying Land Deeds], *Hürriyet*, 11 April 2003, 1; and "24 Saatlik Kerkük Kabusu" [Nightmare of 24 Hours in Kirkuk], *Radikal*, 11 April 2003, 1.

58   Daniel Williams, "Rampant Looting Sweeps Iraq," *Washington Post*, 12 April 2003, A01.

59   Taylor (2004), 125.

60   Dexter Filkins, "Lands Taken by Saddam Reclaimed by Kurds," *International Herald Tribune*, 21 June 2004, 5.

61   For more on this topic, see Human Rights Watch report, "Claims in Conflict: Reversing Ethnic Cleansing in Northern Iraq," New York, 3 August 2004 at http://hrw.org/reports/2004/iraq0804/iraq0804.pdf.

62   Associated Press News Agency, 16 September 2004.

63   Richard Oppel Jr., "Kurds Seek to Maintain a Fragile Autonomy," *International Herald Tribune*, 3 January 2005, 2.

64   Peter Galbraith, "As Iraqis Celebrate, the Kurds Hesitate," *International Herald Tribune*, 2 February 2005, 6. Galbraith is a former United States ambassador to Croatia and is currently an adviser to Iraqi Kurds.

65   An Ottoman administrative unit meaning county or subdistrict.

66   For an insightful account of this period in the political history of northern Iraq, see Sinan Marufoğlu, *Osmanlı Döneminde Kuzey Irak* [Northern Iraq in Ottoman Era] (İstanbul: Eren Yayıncılık, 1998), 31-40. For cogent assessments of Kirkuk's civic and administrative lives at the turn of the twentieth century, see Ebubekir Hazım Tepeyran, *Hatıralar* [Recollections], 2nd ed. (İstanbul: Pera Turizm ve Ticaret, 1998), 505-512. In fact, the book is more nearly a work of analytical research than a memoir. Tepeyran, a professional administrator, served as governor of the Mosul province from 1899 to 1902.

67   Tepeyran (1998), 358-362 and 521-527.

68   Documents on British Foreign Policy, 1919-1939, Llewellyn Woodward and Rohan Butler eds. (London: Her Majesty's Stationery Office, 1960). 1st ser.,vol. 4, appendix 10 to no. 426, Memorandum concerning the new organisation of

the Ottoman Empire, 23 June 1919, 647-651. For the full text of the Fourteen Points see Papers Relating to the Foreign Affairs of the United States. The Paris Peace Conference, 1919. (Washington DC: United States Government Printing Office, 1943). Vol. 4:12-17.

[69]   The full text of the English translation of the Turkish National Pact is contained in J.C. Hurewitz (Ed.), *Diplomacy in the Near and Middle East: A Documentary Record 1914-1956*, vol. 2, (Princeton, NJ: Van Nostrand, 1956), 74-75.

[70]   Baskın Oran, ed., *Türk Dış Politikası 1919-1980* [Turkish Foreign Policy 1919-1980], vol.1 (İstanbul: İletişim Yayınları, 2001), 261 and 263. Also see "The Iraq Dispute: Note and Map", *Foreign Affairs*, vol. 3, no. 4 (July 1925), 687-688.

[71]   Text of the treaty in Great Britain, Treaty Series. Turkey No. 1 (1926). Treaty between the United Kingdom and Iraq and Turkey regarding the Settlement of the Frontier between Turkey and Iraq together with Notes exchanged, Ankara, June 5, 1926. Command Papers 2679 (London: His Majesty's Stationery Office, 1926).

[72]   See FO 371 E2957/62/65. Negotiations regarding Mosul: oil royalties question. Austen Chamberlain (FO) to Ronald Lindsay (Ankara), 17 May 1926.

[73]   See Article 10 of the Convention, Made at London on 14 March 1925, between the Turkish Petroleum Company and the government of Iraq (London: Blundell, Taylor and Com., 1925).

[74]   See, for instance, among others FO 371 E2965/62/65. Mosul oil royalties. Minute (James Morgan), 13 May 1926, and Colonial Office Papers, National Archives, Kew, London (henceforth referred to as CO) 9862/26. Letter from CO to FO forwarding the telegram of Henry Dobbs (Baghdad) to the Secretary of State for the Colonies, 10 May 1926.

[75]   To name a few, see Mehmet Gönlübol and Cem Sar, *Olaylarla Türk Dış Politikası 1919-1965* [Turkish Foreign Policy Through Events 1919-1965] (Ankara: Siyasal Kitabevi, 1996), 72; Oral Sander, *Siyasi Tarih 1918-1994* [Political History 1918-1994] (Ankara: İmge Kitabevi, 2004), 99; Erik Zürcher, *Turkey: A Modern History* (London: I. B. Tauris, 1993), 210; Andrew Mango, *Atatürk* (London: John Murray, 1999), 443; and William Hale, *Turkish Foreign Policy 1774-2000* (London: Frank Cass, 2000), 76n.33.

[76]   See Hikmet Uluğbay, *İmparatorluktan Cumhuriyete Petropolitik* [Petropolitics From Empire to Republic] (Ankara: Turkish Daily News Yayınları, 1995), 261-262. Also Yücel Güçlü, Türkiye'nin Irak Petrol Gelirlerinden 25 Yıl Süreyle Yüzde 10 Hisse Alacaklarının Bakiyesi [The Remaining Dues Accruing to Turkey From Its 10 Percent Share for a Period of Twenty-five Years of Iraq's Oil Revenues], 31 March 2003. Unpublished paper in Turkish.

77   India Office Records, British Library, Euston, London. Political and Secret
     Department (henceforth referred to as IO). L/P.S/10/619. P. 3540 1919
     Portion (1) Mesopotamia. Kirkuk Progress Report, No. 2, For period ending
     29 November 1918. Assistant Political Officer for Kirkuk Stephen Hemsley
     Longrigg.
78   IO. L/P.S/129/19. P. 4322. Administration Report of the Kirkuk Division for
     the period 1 January-31 December 1919.
79   IO. L/P.S/Mesopotamia: Proceedings of the Kirkuk Divisional Council.
     P. 2023/1919. Memorandum No. K.1760/3/1 of 26 November 1919
     from Political Officer, Kirkuk, to the Civil Commissioner, Baghdad, with
     enclosures.
80   Air Ministry Papers, National Archives, Kew, London (henceforth referred
     to as AIR) 23/388.I/14/15. Special Service Officer (British Air Intelligence)
     Kirkuk, 27 November 1925.
81   Cecil John Edmonds, *Kurds, Turks and Arabs: Politics, Travel and Research in
     North-Eastern Iraq 1919-1925* (London: Oxford University Press, 1957), 282.
     A Turkish translation exists. Edmonds, of the British Levant Consular Service,
     corps of Middle Eastern language specialists, was brought up from Bushire
     in Iran where he had been vice-consul to serve as Administrative Inspector in
     Kirkuk in 1922-1925 and later act as adviser to the Ministry of the Interior
     of Iraq, 1935-1945. Also Stephen Hemsley Longrigg, *Iraq 1900 to 1950: A
     Political, Social, and Economic History*, 2nd ed. (London: Oxford University
     Press, 1956), 127.
82   Philip Willard Ireland, *Iraq: A Study in Political Development* (London: Jonathan
     Cape, 1937), 284. On the personality and activities of İzzet Paşa of Kirkuk see
     also Hürmüzlü (2003), 21 and 43 and Saatçı (2003), 192. As yet no biography
     of this Turcoman statesman is written. He deserves one. It should attempt
     to portray the man and to place his career in perspective against the historic
     unfolding of the events in which he took part.
83   Private Papers of Cecil John Edmonds, Middle Eastern Centre at St. Antony's
     College, Oxford. (henceforth referred to as Edmonds Papers) Box 1, File
     1A, Monthly Reports on Kirkuk for the period 1-31 July and 1-31 August
     1921.
84   Christopher Catherwood, *Winston's Folly* (London: Constable and Robinson,
     2004). As the book's title indicates, much blame is assigned to British policy.
85   Liora Lukitz, *Iraq: The Search for National Identity* (London: Frank Cass,
     1995), 40. Lukitz holds that the modern Iraqi state system is merely a veneer
     over tribal and communal identities and finds that the past one hundred years
     of Iraqi history have failed to change primordial allegiances in meaningful

ways. For more recent scholarship on the creation of the modern Iraqi state see Toby Dodge, *Inventing Iraq: The Failure of Nation Building and a History Denied* (New York: Columbia University Press, 2003). Dodge, a political sociologist, depicts Iraq as a failed state arising from failed British policies and administrations early in the twentieth century. He argues that an analysis of the mandatory period provides the key to understanding the current malaise in Iraq.

86   D. K. Fieldhouse, ed., *Kurds, Arabs and Britons: The Memoir of Wallace Lyon in Iraq, 1918-1941* (London: I. B. Tauris, 2002), 107. Lyon served twenty-three years as administrative inspector and adviser in Mosul, Dohuk, Arbil, and Kirkuk during and after the British mandate.

87   Arnold Wilson, *Mesopotamia, 1917-1920: A Clash of Loyalties* (London: Oxford University Press, 1931), 259-260. Wilson's book is largely a memoir of his years in Baghdad.

88   Edmonds Papers, Box 1, Secret No. K361, Edmonds, political officer at Kirkuk, to Kinahan Cornwallis, adviser to the Ministry of the Interior, 2 July 1923 and 22 October 1923.

89   Edmonds Papers, Box 3, File 2, Edmonds, political officer at Kirkuk, to Charles Hooper, adviser to the Ministry of Justice, 16 March 1929.

90   FO 371/1008. Gerald Lowther (Istanbul) to Edward Grey (London) with enclosures and annexes, 5 April 1910, notes on Mosul district. Enclosure 2 in No. 1. Notes by Vice-Consul Wilkie Young on the Mosul district, paragraphs 16 and 80.

91   FO 371/5081. Extract from report prepared by Gertrude Bell under direction of civil commissioner, Baghdad. Mesopotamia: Review of Civil Administration, 1914-1918, 47 and 51.

92   David Oates, *Studies in the Ancient History of Northern Iraq* (London: Oxford University Press, 1968), 16.

93   Nelida Fuccaro, *The Other Kurds: Yazidis in Colonial Iraq* (London: I. B. Tauris, 1999), 32-33.

94   See, among others, "Talafar Blockade Is Lifted After Turks Protest to United States," *International Herald Tribune*, 15 September 2004, 6; Rick Jervis, "Uprooted Residents Return After Revolt," *Chicago Tribune*, 15 September 2004, 4; Rick Jervis, "Clash Opens New Front for Rebels; Fight for Key Northern Town Proved Intense," *South Florida Sun-Sentinel*, 15 September 2004, 20A; Edward Wong, "Three Decapitated Bodies Found; Two Men Are Killed in Bombing," *The New York Times*, 16 September 2004, A12; and Rick Jervis, "United States General Visits Besieged City," *Chicago Tribune*, 17 September 2004, 6.

95   Jonathan Finer, "5,000 United States and Iraqi Troops Sweep Into City of Talafar; Urban Assault Is Largest Since Last Year," *Washington Post,* 3 September 2005, A25.

96   William Rupert Hay, *Two Years in Kurdistan: Experiences of a Political Officer 1918-1920* (London: Sidgwick and Jackson, 1921), 81 and 85-86.

97   Private Papers of William Rupert Hay, Middle Eastern Centre at St.Antony's College, Oxford. Mesopotamia 1917-1922. Monthly Reports, Arbil Division, December 1920.

98   Edmonds (1957), 265 and 278.

99   Lausanne Conference Records, 373-374.

100 Ibid., 342.

101 Article 3, paragraph 2 of the Lausanne Treaty ran as follows: "The frontier between Turkey and Iraq shall be laid down in friendly arrangement to be concluded between Turkey and Britain within nine months. In the event of no agreement being reached between the two governments within the time mentioned, the dispute shall be referred to the Council of the League of Nations. The Turkish and British governments reciprocally undertake that, pending a decision to be reached on the subject of the frontier, no military or other movement shall take place which might modify in any way the present state of the territories of which the final fate will depend upon that decision." Full text of the treaty in League of Nations Treaty Series, vol. 28, no. 14 (1924), 111-14.

102 League of Nations, report submitted to the Council by the commission instituted by the Council Resolution of 30 September 1924, Document C. 400, M-147, 1925, VII, 5 and 38.

103 Ibid., 38 and 47-48.

104 Ibid., 38.

105 Hanna Batatu, *The Old Social Classes and the Revolutionary Movements of Iraq: A Study of Iraq's Old Landed and Commercial Classes and of Its Communists, Baathists, and Free Officers* (Princeton, NJ: Princeton University Press, 1978), 913. The author gives Iraq, Ministry of the Interior, *Statistical Compilation Relating to the Population Census of 1957* (in Arabic), I, Part IV, 170 as his source. David McDowall in *A Modern History of the Kurds* (London: I. B. Tauris, 1996), 3 concurs on this and in page 329 mentions that "the 1957 census showed that the Turcomans were predominant in Kirkuk."

106 For a discussion, see Marion Farouk-Sluglett and Peter Sluglett, *Iraq Since 1958: From Revolution to Dictatorship* (London: I. B. Tauris, 1990), 71.

107 Aslı Aydıntaşbaş, "One Iraqi Obstacle You Haven't Heard Of," *The New Republic,* 8 July 2002, 29. For a fuller discussion of this affair see the chapter after the next.

[108]   Text of the treaty in Treaty Series No. 15 (1931), Treaty of Alliance between His Majesty in respect of the United Kingdom and His Majesty the King of Iraq, with an exchange of notes, Baghdad, 30 June 1930. Command Papers 3797 (London: His Majesty's Stationery Office, 1931).

[109]   CO 730/152, File 78058. Minute (Hall), 26 July 1930.

[110]   League of Nations, Permanent Mandates Commission, Minutes of the Twenty-first Session, 26 October-13 November 1931, 1.

[111]   Ibid., 2.

[112]   Ibid., 110.

[113]   CO 730/162, File 88058. Minute (Hall), 4 June 1931; FO 371/16028. E369/9/93. Departmental memorandum, 21 January 1932.

[114]   Text of the Declaration of the Kingdom of Iraq, Made in Baghdad on 30 May 1932, on the occasion of the termination of the mandatory regime in Iraq, and containing the guarantees given to the council by the Iraqi government will be found in Appendix II.

[115]   See League of Nations document, C.444.1932.VI dated 30 May 1932.

[116]   For the assumption of the United Nations of the functions and powers belonging to the League of Nations under the international agreements, see League of Nations, *Official Journal*, Records of the Twentieth (Conclusion) and Twenty-first Ordinary Sessions of the Assembly, Texts of the Debates at the Plenary Meetings and Minutes of the First and Second Committees, Special Supplement No. 194, 1946, 221-224. For the transfer to the United Nations of certain functions and activities of the League of Nations, see Yearbook of the United Nations 1946-1947 (Lake Success, NY: Department of Public Information, 1947), 110-113.

[117]   Peter Sluglett, *Britain in Iraq, 1914-1932* (London: Ithaca Press, 1976), 182-194. Also see Cecil John Edmonds, "The Kurds of Iraq," *Middle East Journal*, vol. 11, no. 2 (Winter 1957): 59 and, by the same author, "The Kurds and Revolution in Iraq," *Middle East Journal*, vol. 13, no. 1 (Winter 1959): 10.

[118]   Necmettin Esin, "Tarihi Bir Türk Şehri: Kerkük" [A Historic Turkish City: Kirkuk], *Türk Kültürü*, vol. 12, no. 135 (January 1974): 195-199. For a more recent treatment of the subject see Oktay Ekinci, "Kerkük İçin Susanlara" [To Those Who Remain Silent on Kirkuk], *Cumhuriyet*, 3 February 2005, 15. Ekinci is one of the preeminent authorities on Iraqi Turcoman architecture. He has spent over three decades of doing scholarly work, writing, lecturing, and teaching.

[119]   Reader Bullard, *The Camels Must Go* (London: Faber and Faber, 1961), 100.

[120]   Private Papers of Reader Bullard, Middle Eastern Centre at St. Antony's College, Oxford. Box 3, File 3, Mesopotamian diary.

121   Julian Borger, "United States Occupation Plan Sidelines Iraqi Exiles," *Guardian*, 12 October 2002, 8.

122   "Iraqi Kurds Demand Right to Own and Manage Northern Oil Reserves," *Middle East Economic Survey*, vol. 157, no. 24 (14 June 2004): A4. Text of the transitional administrative law is available at http://www.cpa-iraq.org/government/TAL.html.

123   "Revenue from Future Iraqi Kurdistan Oil Finds Must Be for Kurds, Says Barzani. DNO Accord," *Middle East Economic Survey*, vol. 157, No. 27 (5 July 2004): A8-A9.

124   Ibid., A9.

125   "Iraq Warns International Oil Companies Against Circumventing Central Government in Oil Talks," *Middle East Economic Survey*, vol. 157, no. 29 (19 July 2004): A3-A4.

126   Associated Press News Agency, 30 December 2004.

127   "Northern Challenge," *Middle East Economic Survey*, vol. 157, no. 41 (11 October 2004): A4.

128   "Heritage Oil Joins List of International Oil Companies Pursuing Ventures in Iraqi Kurdistan," *Middle East Economic Survey*, vol. 157, nos. 51-52 (20-27 December 2004): A14.

129   Ibid., A14-A15.

130   Steve Fainaru and Anthony Shadid, "Kurdish Officials Sanction Abductions in Kirkuk; United States Memo Says, Turcomans Secretly Sent to North," *Washington Post*, 15 June 2005, A01.

131   Ibid.

132   Ibid.

133   George Kirk, *Contemporary Arab Politics: A Concise History* (New York: Frederick Praeger, 1961), 162-163. See also, Foreign Relations of the United States. Diplomatic Papers (1958-1960). (Washington DC: State Department, 1993). Vol. 12, 473-495. One of the most recent and best Turcoman treatments of this subject is to be found in the first chapter of Şemsettin Küzeci's study, *Kerkük Soykırımları* [Kirkuk Genocides] (Ankara: Teknoed Yayınları, 2004), 49-107. The book deserves an annotated English translation for the use of specialists in Middle Eastern affairs. Küzeci is an Ankara-based journalist and broadcaster who began his career in Kirkuk and Baghdad.

134   FO 371 E1015/426. Turks attacked and killed by Kurds in Kirkuk. Humphrey Trevelyan (Baghdad) to FO, 20 July 1959. It is significant that the British ambassador in his correspondence with London prefers to use the name Turks instead of Turcomans. His account is that of a trained, interested observer of this critical period of intense domestic turmoil in northern Iraq. Trevelyan, in

his memoirs, later commented that while the celebrations were continuing on the first anniversary of the revolution in Baghdad, a bloody scene was being enacted in Kirkuk—the town in which there was a strong Turcoman element. According to him, the processions there touched off several days of rioting and murder, almost certainly arranged by Kurdish communists in order to terrorise their old Turcoman enemies. He further noted that the Iraqi premier reacted strongly and, showing photographs of the atrocities at a press conference, virtually accused the communists of being responsible for the outrages. See Humphrey Trevelyan, *The Middle East in Revolution* (London: MacMillan, 1970), 162.

[135] FO 371 E1015/448. Letter from Peter Hayman (Baghdad) to George Hiller (FO) on the Kirkuk massacre and its aftermath, 24 July 1959.

[136] FO 371 E1015/449. Kassem shocked by Kirkuk atrocities. Peter Hayman (Baghdad) to FO, 30 July 1959. It should, however, be realised that Zeki Kuneralp, the deputy secretary-general of the Turkish Ministry of Foreign Affairs had informed the Baghdad Pact Deputies at Ankara on 23 July 1959 that twenty-five Turks had been killed during the Kirkuk massacre. See FO 371 E1015/426. Letter from L. M. Minford (Ankara) to C. M. Le Quesne (FO) on the troubles in Kirkuk, 25 July 1959.

[137] USNA 787.00/7-1759. Incidents at Kirkuk. John Jernegan (Baghdad) to secretary of state, 17 July 1959. Jernegan's reports show that he accurately foresaw some of the long-term problems that Iraq would have to face both domestically and internationally. In retrospect, his concerns were prescient.

[138] USNA 787.00/7-2059. Kassem's speech at the Chaldean church. John Jernegan (Baghdad) to secretary of state, 20 July 1959.

[139] USNA 787.00/7-2359. Incidents at Kirkuk. Flake (London) to secretary of state, 23 July 1959.

[140] USNA 787.00/7-3159. Kassem's press conference. John Jernegan (Baghdad) to secretary of state, 31 July 1959.

[141] USNA 787.00/8-859. Kassem's speech to the representatives of the trade unions and popular organisations. John Jernegan (Baghdad) to secretary of state, 5 August 1959.

[142] USNA 787.00/9-359. Conversation with the Turkish Ministry of Foreign Affairs Officer. Fletcher Warren (Ankara) to secretary of state, 6 August 1959. İleri served as chief of section at the Directorate-General of Second Department of the Turkish Ministry of Foreign Affairs, 1958-1960. He was first secretary of the Turkish embassy at Baghdad between 1955 and 1958. For his biographical details see *Türkiye Cumhuriyeti Dışişleri Bakanlığı 1967 Yıllığı* (1967 Yearbook of the Ministry of Foreign Affairs of the Republic of Turkey)

(Ankara: Ankara Basım ve Ciltevi, 1968), 517. İleri's previous experience in Iraq and regional knowledge served him well in diagnosing the existing phase in Turcoman-Kurdish relations.

143   Phebe Marr, *The Modern History of Iraq* (Boulder, Col.: Westview Press, 1985), 166.

144   For a lengthier discussion of this point, see Majid Khadduri, *Republican Iraq: A Study in Iraqi Politics since the Revolution of 1958* (London: Oxford University Press, 1969), 124. Edgar O'Ballance in *The Kurdish Struggle, 1920-1994* (London: MacMillan, 1996), 40, quoting the *Times* of 30 July 1959, refers that Kassem later admitted that forty had been buried alive.

145   Text of the treaty in Treaty Series No.17 (1925), Treaty of Alliance between Great Britain and Iraq, Baghdad, 10 October 1922. Command Papers 2370 (London: His Majesty's Stationery Office, 1925).

146   AIR 5/1254. Iraq Command Report, April 1924 to November 1926.

147   AIR 23/562. Special Kirkuk, Aviation Baghdad, 10 May 1926; CO, Colonial No. 13, Report by His Britannic Majesty's Government on the Administration of Iraq for the period April 1923-December 1924 (London: His Majesty's Stationery Office, 1925), 36, does not give the number of Turcomans killed in this outbreak. For a Turcoman account of the issue see Saatçı (2003), 193-195. Also Yenerer (2004), 119-120.

148   Article 27 of the International Covenant on Civil and Political Rights declares that "in those states in which ethnic, religious or linguistic minorities exist, persons belonging to such minorities shall not be denied the right, in community with the other members of their group, to enjoy their own culture, to profess and practice their own religion, or to use their own language." The covenant was adopted and opened for signature, ratification and accession by United Nations (henceforth referred to as UN) General Assembly resolution 2200A (21) of 16 December 1966. It entered into force on 23 March 1976. Full text is available at http://www.unhchr.ch/html/menu3/6/a_ccpr.htm.

149   UN Economic and Social Council, Commission on Human Rights, Forty-ninth session agenda item 12, Report on the situation of human rights in Iraq, prepared by Max van der Stoel, special rapporteur of the Commission on Human Rights in accordance with Commission resolution 1992/71, E/CN.4/1993/45, 19 February 1993, 4.

150   UN General Assembly, Forty-sixth session agenda item 98 (c), Situation of human rights in Iraq: Note by the Secretary-General, A/46/647, 13 November 1991, 69.

151   UN Economic and Social Council, Commission on Human Rights, Forty-eighth session agenda item 12, Report on the situation of human rights in

Iraq prepared by the special rapporteur Max van der Stoel in accordance with Commission resolution 1991/74, E/CN.4/1992/31, 18 February 1992, 31.

152 Ibid., 31-32.

153 UN Economic and Social Council, Commission on Human Rights, Forty-ninth session agenda item 12, Report on the situation of human rights in Iraq, prepared by Max van der Stoel, special rapporteur of the Commission on Human Rights in accordance with Commission resolution 1992/71, E/CN.4/1993/45, 19 February 1993, 4.

154 Ibid., 5.

155 Ibid., 8.

156 Ibid., 9.

157 Ibid.

158 Ibid.

159 UN Economic and Social Council, Commission on Human Rights, Forty-ninth session agenda item 12, Report on the situation of human rights in Iraq prepared by the Special Rapporteur Max van der Stoel in accordance with Commission resolution 1992/71, E/CN.4/1993/45, 19 February 1993, 23-24.

160 UN Economic and Social Council, Commission on Human Rights, Fiftieth session agenda item 12, Report on the situation of human rights in Iraq submitted by the Special Rapporteur Max van der Stoel in accordance with Commission resolution 1993/74, E/CN.4/1994/58, 25 February 1994, 48-49.

161 Ibid., 32 and 49.

162 Ibid., 21, 24, and 49.

163 Ibid., 31-32.

164 Ibid., 10, 14, 24, and 48.

165 UN General Assembly, Fifty-first session agenda item 110 (c), Situation of human rights in Iraq: Note by the secretary general, A/51/496/Add.1,8 November 1996, 4. Also see Said Aburish, *Saddam Hussein: The Politics of Revenge* (London: Bloomsbury, 2000), 87 where it is stated that "in 1970 Saddam Hussein began to attempt to change the ethnic make-up of the ever-contested city of Kirkuk to guarantee its eventual control by Arabs. Curiously, though both Arabs and Kurds claimed the city, the majority of its inhabitants were neither Kurds nor Arabs but Turcomans."

166 UN General Assembly, Fifty-first session agenda item 110 (c), Situation of human rights in Iraq: Note by the secretary-general, A/52/476/Add.1,15 October 1997, 2.

167 Ibid., 2-3.

168 UN General Assembly, Commission on Human Rights, Fifty-first session agenda item 10, Report on the violations of human rights in Iraq submitted by the special rapporteur Max van der Stoel in accordance with Commission resolution 1997/60,E/CN.4/1987/67, 10 March 1998, 2.

169 Full text of the United States State Department's 2003 report on human rights in Iraq is available at http://www.state.gov/g/dr/rls/hrrpt/2003/c11109.htm.

170 UN Economic and Social Council, Commission on Human Rights, Fifty-fifth session agenda item 9, Report on the situation of human rights in Iraq submitted by the special rapporteur Max van der Stoel in accordance with Commission resolution 1998/65,E/CN.4/1999/37, 26 February 1999, 7.

171 Ibid., 8.

172 European Parliament, Resolution on the situation in Iraq eleven years after the Gulf war, P5-TA(2002)0248, 16 May 2002, 2-3.

173 Reuters News Agency, 2 March 2004.

174 UN Economic and Social Council, Commission on Human Rights, Sixty-first session item 6(a) of the provisional agenda, Written statement entitled "Racism, racial discrimination, xenophobia and all forms of discrimination: comprehensive implementation of and follow-up to the Durban Declaration and Programme of Action" submitted by the Transnational Radical Party, E/CN.4/2005/NGO/261, 10 March 2005, 3.

175 Ibid.

176 Ibid., 3-4.

177 Ibid., 4.

178 Ibid., 4-5.

INDEX